# A Song For Rio

## KAY ELLIS

ENCOMPASS INK

# Contents

*Chapter One*

ANOTHER HOTEL ROOM. Another hangover. Another stranger in my bed. The fact the body was female made a change. Don't get me wrong. She – whoever she was – was far from being the first woman I had ever slept with, but she was the first in... what? Three years now? It wasn't like it had been a conscious choice to only take guys to bed. Simply that I was presented with more opportunities with the male persuasion.

No, actually... that was totally untrue. I was rich and famous and could take my pick of sexual partners any day of the damn week. Not that I did, despite everyone thinking I was a total man-whore. Once or twice a week – maybe three times – and even then, I had to be blind drunk. Being drunk was one thing I had no problem with. The woman in my bed? I had no memory of meeting her, let alone going back to the hotel with her. Knowing me, I hadn't bothered to learn her name either. What did names matter when I had no intention of ever seeing her again?

I slipped from beneath the covers, careful not to wake the slumbering woman, and gathered up my clothes. Looking around, I realised this was not my hotel room. Technically, I had been in *her* bed as opposed to her being in mine. In a lot of ways, it made things easier. It tended to be less messy when I could quietly slip out of the door, rather than having to call security to remove yet another pissed-off one night stand from my bed. Granted, they were not usually pissed off *until* they realised it was a one-time thing, but still...

My only hope was I knew where I was when I left the hotel. Christ, did I even know what city I was in? I paused, one boot half on and half off my foot while I thought about it. England, definitely. I remembered that much. The tour was over, and we'd come home for some needed down time. Which wasn't necessarily a good thing. If the guys all returned to their respective homes and left me to own devices, I could be anywhere. Could have done anything.

It was Dane's fault entirely. He knew I couldn't be trusted.

"Babe? Where are you going?"

Fuck. I spent too long dithering and now my latest conquest was awake and spewing out vomit-inducing terms of endearment.

"I've... um... got somewhere I need to be."

Like anywhere else but in that room.

"Oh, okay." It was an unexpected response, but I'd take it. Calm indifference was preferable to over-the-top hysteria any day. "Will I see you later?"

Ah. There was that ever-burning question. The one that marked the point at which things started to go rapidly downhill.

"I don't know. I'll probably be busy."

Not the strongest excuse in the book, but previous experience had taught me that being honest all too often ended badly. If I said I was going somewhere specific, people expected an invite. And okay, maybe it would be simpler to admit they were just a one-off fuck, but I hated confrontation. Usually, I had to be drunk to deal with any level of aggravation.

"You've got my number though, right?"

"Yeah, sure."

I hadn't even got her name, so why the hell would I have her phone number? She was kind of passive-aggressive, this one, so the sooner I got out of there the better. Male or female, the quiet ones were always the worst.

"You know, I'd love to meet Dane Black," she said casually. "You could arrange it, couldn't you?"

That was the trouble with being me. Nobody ever wanted me for *me*. All anyone really wanted was my connection to Dane. My best friend, who also happened to be the lead singer of Jaded Intent, one of the biggest rock bands in the world. Being Jaded Intent's guitarist made me a poor second to the big man himself. The thing was, I was all too available, while Dane was a hell of a lot harder to get to.

"You know he's gay?" Damn, the whole world ought to know that little detail by now. Dane was a private person, but he had never hidden his sexuality or his love for his boyfriend, Riley. "I don't think he's ever been with a woman in his life."

"He hasn't met me yet."

She sounded so absurdly confident, as though she might actually believe her own bullshit. As if Dane would have touched my sloppy seconds, even before he was all loved up with Riley.

"He's practically married," I said scornfully. "He wouldn't look at someone like you, even if he was straight and single."

"Someone like me?" Oh, now I had her attention. So much for not being confrontational. "What is that supposed to mean?"

"It means I'm leaving."

"You're just jealous," she called after me as I headed for the door. "Dane Black is more of a man than you'll ever be."

I let the door slam behind me. The fact of the matter was, she was right. I was jealous of Dane, only not for the reason she thought. I wanted to be in the same kind of relationship Dane shared with Riley. For someone to look at me with complete adoration in their eyes, the way Dane and Riley looked at each other.

I thought I had it once. I'd come close with Rio. Only then I found he didn't feel the same way. I rushed it, telling him too soon that I was falling in love with him. Rio hadn't answered. He walked out of the room and out of my life that same night.

Except – he had never been out of my life completely. There was no way he could be when he was the drummer for another band, Carnival, and our paths inevitably crossed from time to time. Most recently, it had been when we both helped out Dane's cousin, CJ, by playing at his career making gigs. It was hard to be around Rio though, with him acting like nothing ever happened between us.

Back then, I had been the one to walk out. I'd promised Dane I would show my face at all three of CJ's gigs, but after Rio showed up on the second night, I couldn't bring myself to stay. Dane was still pissed off with me, conveniently forgetting I had saved the entire show by stepping in to play when the band had lost two guitarists in one fell swoop. The first had been carted off to hospital, and the second was arrested for drugging him. It all got a bit messy after that. Anyway, the point was, I had stepped up to the plate. I'd gone on stage with Rio fucking Darke so CJ could finish his gig. I posed for photos and signed autographs, all with Rio standing a hair's breadth away. And then I left, because having him there was tearing me to pieces and nobody – least of all Rio – seemed to notice.

God, it was no wonder I drank as much as I did. My fondness for alcohol was a real bone of intention between Dane and I, but it gave him one more reason to be mad at me. I'd given him enough of those over the years, but then I was nothing if not generous.

Stepping outside the entrance to the hotel, I realised I was about to give him another reason, because I didn't have a clue where I was. The name of the hotel meant nothing to me and there were no familiar landmarks that I could see. I could be anywhere in the country. It bothered me more than I was prepared to admit that I couldn't remember where I'd been the night before.

There was always the option of going back into the hotel and asking the receptionist where the hell I was. Unfortunately, being Garrison Swann meant even the smallest of misdemeanours was newsworthy. Apparently – and I couldn't for the life of me imagine why – where I spent my nights, who I was with and whether I was too pissed to find my way home, was of great interest to Joe Public. So, no – Garrison Swann did not simply walk up to a stranger and announce the fact he didn't know where the fuck he was.

Pulling the hood of my sweatshirt up to hide my all-too-famous face, I jogged across the road to a small public garden with benches. Casual clothes were a good thing, I thought, glancing down at my faded jeans and scruffy trainers. Casual meant I had not come from an interview or some big, fancy charity event. Not remembering where I'd been was a definite problem though. My memory was getting worse and when Dane figured it out, he would ship me off for another stint in rehab that I really didn't need. I was in perfect control of my drinking, thank you very much.

Sitting on one of the benches, I took my phone from my pocket. Thank God I hadn't lost the thing again. Last time I mislaid it, every famous face on my contact list had to change their number and none of them had been pleased about it. My name was mud for weeks – months even – and there were quite a few of them who had refused to give me their new number until I sorted my life out. Whatever *that* was supposed to mean.

Dane, however, could not withhold his number for obvious reasons, so he was the lucky one whose phone I called. Annoyingly, Riley answered. I had nothing against the man, but ever since they met, I'd slipped further down the list of importance in Dane's eyes. Riley was a nice guy. Everyone said as much, so I guess it must be true. Sometimes, though, I got the impression he didn't entirely approve of me. Deep down, I knew it had more to do with my close relationship to Dane than my personality, but either way – Riley was not my biggest fan.

"My battery is low," I said abruptly, not bothering to say hello. "Get Dane. I need to speak to him."

"No."

"What the fuck, Riley? Just put him on the phone."

"I said no. He's been up half the night trying to find you. I'm not waking him."

"I'm fine. I went to... visit a friend," I lied pathetically. I didn't even sound convincing to my own ears, so someone smart like Riley was never going to buy that line of bullshit. "He needn't have worried."

"Right. You don't show up for the radio interview or answer your phone or any of the fifty thousand messages he sent you, but it's nothing to worry about," Riley answered scornfully. "I'll be sure to let Dane know."

Just like that, the little bastard hung up on me. I would wring his bloody neck when I saw him. And I was still none the wiser as to my location. What was he blathering on about anyway? A radio interview? Since when? Well... since last night evidently. How could I have forgotten?

Looking at my phone, I noticed I did indeed have a long list of missed calls and unread text messages from Dane. Not quite the fifty thousand Riley claimed, but definitely in to double figures.

I didn't have time to call anyone else before my battery died. Who would I call anyway? I was not as close to the other guys as I was to Dane, so it was unlikely they would come even if I asked them to. KP was on some sort of spiritual retreat and probably didn't have his phone on him anyway. Hey, I remembered that much, so my memory was not a total loss. Unlike my phone, which was now just a useless lump of plastic in my hand.

I shoved it back into my pocket with a growl of frustration. It looked as though I would have to start walking and hope I eventually stumbled across some place I recognised.

I hadn't gone all that far when I reached a train station, so I now knew I was in Swindon. What the hell was I doing in Swindon? Well... a radio interview, apparently, even though I'd missed it. But how could I not have known? Dane and Riley would blame it on the booze, but whatever they thought, I was not an alcoholic. I controlled the booze. It didn't control me. I could stop any time I wanted to.

*Yeah, keep telling yourself that. Saying it doesn't make it true.*

The memory lapses were a slight concern, but they would go away if I laid off the alcohol for a few days. It wouldn't bother me. Just because I liked a drink didn't mean I *needed* it to get me through the day. Not that anyone ever believed me.

*I believe me. Otherwise, what's the point of carrying on?*

Suddenly, it occurred to me that I didn't want to go home. I didn't want to be found and be subjected to endless lectures from all and sundry about my behaviour. I didn't care if they finally decided to kick me out of Jaded Intent, because I wasn't sure I wanted to be in the band anyway. I was sick and tired of being Garrison Swann. Sick of living my life in the public eye, which people seemed to think gave them the right to judge me.

Like an epiphany, it struck me. I could stop. I didn't have to be that person anymore. I could get on a train and go anywhere. Be anyone who wasn't Garrison Swann. I could even try being me for a while.

Trouble was, it had been so long, I didn't know who *me* was.

# Chapter Two

A MERE FIVE HOURS LATER, I was in Dartmouth. I wish I
could say it was a spur of the moment decision, a subconscious choice
from the departures board. But if I was serious about embarking on this
journey of self-discovery, I had to start by being honest with myself.
From the moment I spotted Dartmouth on the board, I hadn't contem-
plated going any place else.

There was still a fair way to go before I reached the place I intended
to stay and I had to figure out transport for the final leg of the journey,
but I felt a sense of achievement at having got as far as I had. Look at me,
taking responsibility and adulting and stuff. Anyone would think I was
a proper grown-up.

The biggest problem I had now was that although I knew where I
was going, I didn't know the address. In fact, I didn't even know the
name of the village, so a taxi was out of the question. For once it had
nothing to do with my shockingly bad memory either. Rio had taken
me there for a few days during our fling and I was so happy to be with
him, I never thought to ask where we were. And seeing as we spent most
of the time in bed, I hadn't exactly had a guided tour of the area.

Come to think of it, we had not entered the village by road, so I wouldn't have seen a place name anyway. Rio had parked his fancy car in a private garage and hired a boat to ferry us along the river. We'd approached the cottage from the water.

I walked along the quay, eyeing the boats hopefully. It was three years since I was last here. The boat might have changed, or the owner might have retired. Or died. He seemed pretty ancient at the time, so it wouldn't surprise me. I was grasping at straws really, thinking he would still be around.

But just as I was about to admit defeat, spied an old man sat in a deckchair on the quayside. I was as certain as I could be that it was him. There was I, worrying things would have changed over the past three years, and there was him, looking like he was wearing the same old jumper and stained trousers as he had back then.

He watched me through disinterested eyes as I walked over to him.

"Do you remember me?" I asked.

"No, but let me guess," he said, looking me up and down with a sneer. "You're one of Mr. Darke's male companions."

Ouch. I mean, I wasn't stupid. I knew I wasn't Rio's one and only. It wasn't like he was mine either, but I thought I was the only one he'd ever taken to his secret hideaway. It was what he told me at the time, and I'd believed him. Clearly, I was one of many and didn't *that* sting way more than it should?

"So, will you take me out there?"

"Nope. Don't think I will," he answered smugly.

"Why not? I can pay."

"I dare say you can, but that's not the point, is it? Mr. Darke never told me anyone was coming, and I can't just go schlepping people out there, can I? Not when it's his house."

"He's expecting me," I lied, out of sheer desperation. "He's meeting me at the cottage."

"Maybe he is and maybe he ain't," the old man answered with the kind of smirk that made me want to smack it clean off his wrinkled face. "Don't make no difference. Come back here with Mr. Darke and then I'll take you."

"Fuck you!" I snapped hotly. "If you can afford to turn down two hundred quid for a couple of hours' work, good for you. Oh, and for the record, when I see Rio tomorrow, I'm going to insist he uses someone else to take us up the river from now on. I'm sure you're not the only guy around here with a boat for hire. You know what? I'm rich. I'll buy my own fucking boat."

He gave me an appraising look, probably trying to decide if I really was important enough to influence Rio, followed by a swift calculation as to whether I actually had any money. Admittedly, my current appearance must make the latter look rather unlikely.

"I want three hundred," he said eventually. "Cash."

"I'm offering you two. Take it or leave it."

"Two fifty," he countered. "And I won't tell Mr. Darke you're here."

"Bye."

I turned on my heel and made to walk away. As I anticipated, I had only taken a few steps before he called me back.

"Okay. Two hundred, but it only buys you a one-way trip along the river. It doesn't buy my silence."

"Fair enough."

To be honest, I wasn't too worried about him telling tales to Rio or anyone else. I seriously doubted he had Rio's number anyway. Rio was careful about shit like that. I bet he only called the guy from a withheld number. And if I remembered correctly, the old man dropped us off at the end of a wooden jetty. He probably didn't know which house was Rio's. Plus, he clearly didn't recognise me, so it wasn't as if he would be in the pub later, blabbing to all his mates about taking Garrison Swann for a ride. In more ways than one. I would hazard a guess he didn't charge Rio two hundred pounds for a forty-five-minute boat trip.

"Is there a cashpoint anywhere nearby? What?" I asked when he shot me a dry look. "I don't carry that much cash on me. Who does these days?"

I half-expected him to demand more money for the information. He thought about it, but then common sense won out. Asking for more money would be pushing his luck, with the very real chance I would simply walk away, and he would end up with nothing.

"Over there," he grumbled, pointing a gnarled finger at a point further along the quay, it wasn't entirely helpful, but it was the most I was going to get without paying through the nose for it.

Once he had his money in his grubby little hand, we began the journey along the river Dart. Sitting at the back of the small boat, I was glad for the loud vibration of the chugging engine that rendered conversation impossible. The old guy was not someone I wanted to talk to anyway, and I guess he was of the same opinion as he stared steadfastly ahead for the entirety of the trip.

I jumped off the boat and onto the small jetty and he disappeared back the way he came with a surprising turn of speed, as if he was afraid I would change my mind and demand to be taken back. Maybe I would have done, given the chance, because I was beginning to realise I had not thought this through at all. So, I made it. Big whoop. What the hell did I do next? I was literally up the creek without a paddle. I had no clean clothes, no food and effectively no phone until I could find a way to charge it.

Rio's house was bound to be locked up tight and even if I was able to break in, I didn't know if there would be any electricity. If he didn't use it that often, he might shut everything down when he wasn't in residence.

Except... he did use it regularly, didn't he? It was where he brought his sexual conquests. Gullible idiots like me, each of us believing we were the only one. That we were something special. All of us kidding ourselves, because the only person Rio Darke gave a shit about was Rio Darke.

A light rain started to fall, and a cold breeze blew in from the water, making me shiver. I tucked my hands inside my hoodie. I was not going to find any answers by freezing to death on the dock, so I carefully made my way along the slippery wooden planks and up the sandy embankment to what was basically Rio's front garden.

At least I didn't have to worry about being seen lurking because there were no immediate neighbours. There were other homes further back, but Rio's was the only one on the water's edge, on this quiet little corner of the river anyway.

I guess the house was a fisherman's cottage at one point. Rio had modernised the interior extensively, but the outside remained old fashioned and rustic in appearance. Not what people would expect from someone like Rio, which was probably why he chose it. Nobody would ever believe the humble abode was home to one of rock music's biggest stars.

After Dozer, of course. And Phil Collins. Tico Torres. Roger Taylor. That guy from Def Leppard with one arm. Rio was right up there with the greats, even if he wasn't top of the list.

I walked around the cottage, looking for a way in. I didn't want to cause any damage by smashing a window. Not because it was Rio's property – I didn't give a toss about that – but because the whole place was as silent as the grave and the sound of breaking glass would carry for miles. The last thing I needed was some well-intentioned neighbour sticking their nose where it wasn't wanted.

Nor did I want to cut myself and end up bleeding to death. I wanted to disappear for a while, but I didn't want to die. At least, I didn't think I did. I was pissed off with life in general, but I wasn't suicidal.

The patio furniture was neatly stacked against the side of the house and covered with a tarpaulin. That was another good sign the house was empty. Rio being here with his latest fuck-toy was something else I hadn't really considered.

I wasted several minutes tugging on window frames and searching under plant pots for hidden door keys, all to no avail. The rain became heavier and before long I was soaked to the skin. I had to make a choice. Walk into the village and beg a complete stranger to take pity on me, or forcibly break-in to the cottage. Either way, I had to do something, sooner rather than later.

A final glance through the window of the back door decided the matter. There was a key in the lock. I couldn't believe Rio could be so careless, or that I hadn't spotted it the first fifty times I peered into the kitchen. The door has a kind of trellis design as well, so I would only have to break one small square of glass. I would pay to have it fixed later.

Stripping off my sodden hoodie, I wrapped it securely around my fist. It took three attempts before I heard a satisfying crack and the sound of broken glass hitting the flagstone floor. It wasn't easy manoeuvring my hand and chunky wrist through the small gap but eventually I managed to turn the key. With a sigh of relief, I opened the door and stepped inside, relieved to be out of the now torrential rain.

Closing the door behind me, I locked it and then removed the key so nobody could pull the same trick as I had just done. I flicked the light switch on the wall, offering up a silent prayer of thanks to whatever god was watching over me when the room flooded with light.

Realising I was starving – unsurprising, since I hadn't eaten in the last twenty-four hours at the very least – I opened the freezer and helped myself to a ready-meal. I should have known the electric would be on, because I suddenly remembered Rio telling me he always kept the freezer stocked so that he only ever needed to bring the basics like bread and milk. So long as he hadn't changed his habits since I was last here, I wasn't going to starve.

I might freeze to death though, especially if I didn't get out of my wet clothes. I threw the frozen chicken curry into the microwave and set the timer, which basically stretched me to the full extent of my cooking skills. Then I toed off my trainers, leaving them to make puddles on the flagstone floor, and made my way upstairs to the bedroom. Originally, the cottage boasted two bedrooms, each the size of a shoebox. Rio had concerted them into one larger bedroom with an en-suite.

Stripping off, I opened the drawer in the large dark wood dresser, searching for dry clothes and socks. Luckily for me, Rio liked to travel light and kept an entire wardrobe at the cottage to avoid having to pack and unpack bags. He was bigger built than me, so everything was a little bit loose, but thankfully the sweatpants I found had a drawstring waist and I was able to tie them tight enough to keep them from slipping. The sleeves of the sweatshirt hung off the ends of my arms, but I could live with that. At least I was warm.

I returned to the kitchen. The microwave was counting down the final two minutes of cooking time, so while I waited, I sieved through the drawers in the hopes of coming across a phone charger. I didn't find one, but I wasn't too disappointed. Giving people a means of contacting me kind of defeated the point of going incommunicado. Dane would be going apeshit trying to find me, but I wasn't there to witness it, so it wasn't my problem. Let Riley deal with it. Serve him right for hanging up on me.

What I did find was an expensive bottle of wine and a corkscrew. Wine was not really to my taste. I preferred beer and spirits, but it wasn't like I had a choice. It would do to wash down the curry. I would undoubtedly have a hangover in the morning, which was another reason I didn't care for wine.

But, hey... it wasn't as if I had any place to be.

# Chapter Three

I WOKE WITH A THICK HEAD, a furry tongue, and a general sensation of someone having taken a pickaxe to my skull. I had no regrets. Turned out, I rather liked wine after all, although the second half of the bottle tasted decidedly better than the first.

Weak light filtered through a gap in the curtains, but I was in no hurry to leave Rio's big comfortable bed. What did I have to get up for anyway? I was warm and cosy beneath the heavy king-size duvet.

I snuggled deeper under the cover and gave thought to what I was going to do with myself during my illicit stay. Tempting as it seemed, I had to do more than drink my way through Rio's wine collection. First on the list was sleeping off this damn hangover, but then what? Sitting on the jetty and watching the boats go by might be nice. Therapeutic even. I would want a disguise in case anyone passed by close enough to recognise me, but I would need to wrap up anyway. It was still cold, even if the rain had dried up.

I might even read for a bit. There was bookcase in the living room, crammed full of every genre imaginable. Rio didn't seem the type to read, but obviously he did. Unless the bookcase was all for show, of course, which seemed unlikely as this was where he came to be himself.

No pretence necessary. God, I couldn't remember the last time I read a book. Probably not for ten years or more by my reckoning.

Sleeping off last night's drinking session was becoming a more elusive feat by the minute. I was too awake. My mind too active.

Resigned to starting my boat-watching, book-reading day several hours earlier than I would have liked, I got out of bed and plodded into the bathroom. I was still wearing my borrowed clothes because it was too cold to take them off until I figured out how to turn on the heating. I didn't bother to wash. There was nobody around to be offended by my body odour, so it seemed pointless.

Fresh breath and clean teeth were a different matter, though. I helped myself to the toothbrush in a mug beside the sink. The mug had the Jaded Intent logo on which had me staring at it stupidly for way too long. Rio wasn't in Jaded Intent. He was in Carnival. So, either the mug was a memento from when he filled in for Dozer or Rio was taking the piss. Yeah, that was the most likely reason he had it. He was mocking me by using my band's mug to hold his toothbrush. Admittedly, a mug I wasn't supposed to see in a house I wasn't supposed to be in.

I scrubbed my teeth extra hard, as though doing so would teach Rio some sort of lesson. Not that he would ever know I'd used his toothbrush. Even if he did find out, he didn't ought to mind. He'd had my dick in his mouth enough times without complaining, so sharing spit shouldn't be an issue.

Suddenly, my nostrils twitched. I could smell fresh coffee. How was that possible? There were no windows open, and no neighbours close enough for the aroma to waft over from another house. It was too strong to be coming from outside anyway. If I was any judge at all, the smell was coming from downstairs... which meant I was well and truly busted.

I crept back into the bedroom and peered out of the window. A blood-red, 69 Corvette Stingray was parked outside. Fuck. Fuck. Fuck. Rio was here. He must have noticed the broken glass in the back door, so why hadn't he called the police or searched the cottage for intruders? Why hadn't he stormed into the bedroom and confronted me? Did he know it was me? And the fact he had driven to the cottage in his car – was that significant?

My heart was in my throat as I descended the narrow staircase. I was not worried about Rio hitting me. If he did, I would hit him right back. But this was the first time we would be alone together since our short-lived and ill-fated affair. I'd seen him a few times in the three years since, but only ever with other people around. It wasn't like we'd engaged in any deep and meaningful conversations. We played on stage together last time I saw him, but I didn't remember saying a single word to him.

He was here alone; I was certain of that. The fact he was here so early and had come in his car was proof that he was not here for a lover's tryst. He was here for a purpose. Namely... me.

I stopped in the kitchen doorway. Rio leaned against the countertop, arms folded, as he waited for the coffee to finish filtering into the pot. There was no such thing as instant coffee in this house. I spent the few short seconds before he noticed me just enjoying the sight of him. I mean, I wasn't bad looking, but Rio was something else. Brilliant blue eyes, full lips, wavy dark-blond hair down to his shoulders, and flawless skin. Even when he looked like he'd been dragged through a hedge backwards, he was fifty shades of gorgeous.

"Mind telling why you broke into my house?"

Shit. As if breaking and entering wasn't bad enough, he had to go and catch me slobbering over him like a deranged stalker.

"It was raining," I said flippantly. "I was getting wet."

"Fair enough," he said, with a small, irritated huff. "But what are you doing here in the first place?"

I shrugged. "Well, I happened to be passing, so..."

"Garrison, stop. This is serious," he snapped. "I could have called the police and had you arrested."

"Then why didn't you?"

"Because..." He turned to face the counter and pour coffee into two waiting mugs. He took a deep, steadying breath before he continued. "Because I knew it was you and I didn't want to give you yet another reason to hate me."

I didn't hate him. I probably never would. It was surprising, though, to learn that he thought I did. That I still wasn't over him three years after he left was testament to the fact my feelings for him were the exact opposite of hate. Telling Rio was out of the question though. Getting too close was the reason he ran out on me in the first place.

"What do you mean, you knew it was me?" I asked as his words sank in. "How did you know?"

"You think I leave this place unprotected?" He raised his eyebrows as he passed me one of the mugs. "There's a silent alarm and motion detection cameras, you idiot, all of which I control from my phone. I've been watching you since you got here. That was a very expensive bottle of wine you necked, by the way."

"Don't worry, I'll pay you back," I said with a scowl, annoyed to discover he was more concerned by the loss of a bottle of bloody wine than anything else he'd seen. If he really had been watching me, it was a good job I'd drunk myself into a stupor before doing anything embarrassing like wank in his bed while calling out his name. I glanced around the kitchen but couldn't see a camera. Wherever it was, it was well hidden. "You know I'm good for the money."

"Not the point, he answered, resuming his laidback position against the counter. "It was vintage and very hard to come by. I was saving it for a special occasion."

"What? You mean next time you bring one of your casual shags here?"

"What are you talking about?" Rio's brow creased in what appeared to be genuine confusion. "You know you're the only man I've ever brought out here. Hell, you're the only one who knows the place even exists."

"Not according to your boat-buddy," I retorted with a snort. Which was just great, because now I sounded like a jealous girlfriend on top of everything else.

"You mean Arthur? You got Arthur to bring you out here?" Rio said, seeming greatly amused by the idea. "How much did he rip you off?"

"Two hundred," I muttered sullenly.

"God, you're such a moron! Don't believe anything that old git tells you. The only time he's happy is when he's causing trouble."

"So... there hasn't been anyone else?" I asked, sounding like a whiny little bitch.

"Don't act dumb," Rio said, eyeing me over the rim of his mug. "There have been a lot of others. I just didn't bring any of them here."

Maybe it was against my better judgement, but I believed him. He had no reason to lie. He didn't like me enough to care whether bringing other men here hurt my delicate feelings.

I groaned and scrubbed a hand across my face. The day was not going as I planned. So much for watching boats and reading a book.

"Did you come all this way to kick me out in person?"

It seemed a bit over the top, especially to have driven through the night as he must have done to be here so early.

"Well, I would have phoned first, but..."

"My phone's dead," I said quickly.

"I was going to say I deleted your number. But yeah. Dead phone. Let's go with that." He smirked, while I shrugged again and pretended not to give a shit. "Anyway, I was enjoying watching you go through every drawer in the house and get wasted on my good wine. I probably would have left you to it, to be honest, although you only had to ask, and I would have brought you down here myself."

"Thanks," I said shortly, "but I got rid of your number too."

I hadn't, but Rio didn't need to know that. A flash of something indefinable streaked across his eyes, but it was gone again before I could figure out what it is. Obviously, though, Rio did not like hearing me say I no longer had his number. In fact, I had lost it when I mislaid my phone, but I stole it back from Dane's contact list when he wasn't looking. Sad as it was, having Rio's number made me feel as though we were still connected on some level. I didn't know why I couldn't let him go when he made it clear he didn't want me, but the situation was what it was.

"If you were so content perving on me from the comfort of your own home," I said, making out he was the one in the wrong for showing up here, "why did you come? Scared I'll drink another bottle of your precious wine?"

"Yeah, that's the only reason," Rio replied with an exaggerated roll of his eyes. "Oh, other than for the fact Dane is going out of his mind trying to find you."

"And what? He called you?"

I couldn't see that happening. Dane was one of the few people who was aware of mine and Rio's brief relationship, but he didn't know the half of it. He didn't know it was love on my part, if not Rio's. And he didn't know Rio had broken my fucking heart the night he left me. But he sure as shit knew Rio was the last person on Earth I would go to for help.

"He called everyone," Rio said dryly. "Including the police."

"Why the fuck would he call the police?"

"To report you missing, dummy." Rio put his mug down on the counter-top before folding his arms again. "The fact you're famous, alcoholic and suicidal makes you a vulnerable person, apparently, so they can skip the whole forty-eight hours thing and start wasting their time and resources straight away."

"I'm not suicidal!"

"But you don't deny being an alcoholic?"

"No! I mean, yes, I deny it." I crossed the kitchen and slammed my empty mug down next to Rio's. "I'm not an alcoholic. I control my drinking. It doesn't control me."

"Said every alcoholic ever since the dawn of time," Rio retaliated swiftly.

"Did you tell Dane where I am?"

"Nope, you can do it yourself."

"No phone, remember?"

God, he was an irritating, arrogant piece of shit. What the hell did I ever see in him? It wasn't like I was attracted by his fame and money. Why would I be, when I had plenty of my own on both counts? He was stupidly good-looking, sure, but what did that matter when his personality sucked?

"I have a charger in the car. You can use that," Rio said.

"I don't want to talk to him. Not yet."

"Don't be such a fucking baby," Rio taunted. "You created this mess, so now you can pull up your big-boy pants and sort it out."

"Fuck you, Rio!"

I went to move away from him, but he caught my wrist in a vice-like grip and pulled me flush against his chest.

"I'd rather fuck you," he said.

# Chapter Four

PUSH HIM AWAY!

My brain screamed at me, even as my body responded to his touch. He hardened against me, and my dick went from soft to rock hard at warp speed. Rio seized my mouth in a ferocious kiss, and I might have moaned into his mouth like a wanton slut as I reciprocated. I wasn't embarrassed. Rio was making enough guttural noises of his own, while he kissed me like his life depended on it.

Besides, I'd waited so long to feel his hands on me again, I couldn't have stopped, whatever my stupid brain tried to tell me.

*He's using you. You're making a mistake. He doesn't mean it. He'll hurt you again.*

Fuck you, brain. It sure as shit felt like he meant it to me. Withing moments, I was face-planted into the wall, with the borrowed sweatpants around my ankles and Rio's fingers prising my cheeks apart and working spit into my arse as lube. I didn't remember crossing the kitchen, but then it didn't matter how we got there. All I cared about was Rio, positioning himself at my entrance.

"Wait..." I panted. "Condom..."

"I'm clean," Rio ground out hoarsely, pushing into me with one hard thrust.

He might be, but what about me? I couldn't remember the last time I got tested, or how many sexual partners I'd had since. Rio was the one taking the risk. Not me. It was his choice, though, and he was already inside me so... *too late.* Not that I had any real intention of stopping him when it felt so good to be joined with him at last.

Rio drove into me, lifting me to the balls of my feet with every upward thrust. I braced my hands against the wall and pushed backwards to meet him. Rio grasped my hips tightly, his pace increasing as he pounded into me without mercy. The sudden realisation that he was only interested in his own release and cared nothing about mine was a painful one. It didn't diminish the pleasure my body was feeling, but my soul was crushed. Well, if Rio wasn't going to oblige, I would literally have to take the matter in hand myself. The emotional fallout could wait until later. Right at that moment, all I wanted was to come.

Resting my forearm on the wall at eye-level, I reached for my dick with my free hand, stroking in tempo with Rio's frantic rhythm. From his laborious breathing, he was close. Which was fine by me because so was I. A few more tugs and I spilled my load into my fist, splattering the paintwork with cum. With a low growl, Rio shoved me into the wall and slammed home four, maybe five times before he was struck by his own shuddering orgasm.

He pulled back my hair and gently kissed the back of my neck, before he realized what he was doing. He stepped away from me, his dick sliding from my arse. He tucked his dick into his jeans, refusing to even look glance in my direction now that he was done with me.

"Pull your pants up," he said shortly. "Then clean that mess off my wall."

"Rio..." I began, not knowing what the hell I was going to say that wasn't going to send him running for the hills. But I had to think of something, because I didn't want it to be this way between us. So we fucked. It wasn't the end of the world. Not for me, at least. It wasn't like I expected him to get down on one knee and propose or anything.

"And call Dane," Rio added brusquely before I could come up with anything even halfway intelligent. "Use my phone if you have to."

He stomped out of the kitchen, as though my very presence offended him. If it was possible for my heart to break any more than it already had, it did so in that moment. I wiped unwelcome tears from my eyes with the sleeve of Rio's hoodie. Fan-fucking-tastic. Now I was crying over Rio-bloody-Darke. Blubbing like a teenage girl over my unrequited love.

Hitching up my sweatpants, I pulled the hoodie over my head and used it to wipe the spunk from the wall. I left pale streaks behind, but I found I didn't care all that much. It was hard to give a shit about anything when the love of my life didn't want me and I couldn't stop fucking crying. Maybe, after I'd gone, the stains would serve as a reminder of what he had lost. Of what he had thrown away because he was an arrogant, selfish prick who was too fucking dense to see how good we could be together.

*That's it, Garrison. Get angry.*

Trouble was, Rio wasn't the one I was most angry with. I loved him. Loved *him* and hated myself. Because – yes, Rio used me – but I didn't exactly put up a fight. I wanted him to fuck me, probably even more than he did, and – if I was honest – I knew how it would end. Yet I dropped my pants for him anyway.

Maybe I was an eternal optimist. Wasn't that the definition of doing the same thing over and over again and expecting a different result? Or was it insanity? It was one or the other. I didn't remember which. Maybe it was both. What did it matter anyway? Rio didn't want me. I gave him my heart and he handed it back in pieces.

Without any real rational thought process, I wandered outside. The day was bright, the weather crisp and cold. Within seconds I was shivering. The thin t-shirt did next to nothing in keeping my upper body warm and my bare feet were all but frozen to the ground.

Despite the cold, however, I didn't want to go back inside. I was not ready to face Rio, or to call Dane and be forced to endure him raging at me over absolutely nothing. Resolving to put off dealing with either of them for as long as humanly possible, I walked around the side of the house and down to the wooden jetty.

An arctic wind swept across the fast-flowing river, and I wrapped my arms around my trembling frame, staring into the murky depths. The water was deep here, the current strong.

How far would it carry my body if I were to drown? How long

before I would be found? Maybe I never would be, and the world would spend a couple of years pondering over the disappearance of Garrison Swann, before confining me to the annals of rock history.

Dane would miss me for a while. Maybe Dozer, KP and Nelson too, but then they would move on. Find a new guitarist. Carry on touring and making music, while I became a distant memory.

Rio wouldn't even feel guilty. He'd just continue shagging his merry way across the known universe, neither knowing nor caring about the devastation he left in his wake. Never feeling one ounce of regret or remorse that he was the one to drive me to this.

But wait. Hold on. Was I seriously considering throwing myself into the river? Had I really reached the point of no return? I mean, I was miserable and hurting, but I'd get over it, wouldn't I? I guess the big question was – did I *want* to stay around long enough to find out if things were going to get better? Or was I tired of waiting for my life to change. Sick of bearing the brunt of everyone's disapproval and disappointment. Weary of being alone. I wanted someone to love me. Someone, who in turn, wanted to spend their life with me, but how was I supposed to find anyone when I was blinded by Rio?

God, so many questions and so few answers. I took a hesitant step closer to the end of the jetty. The water did seem awfully inviting. I could almost hear it calling my name. Tempting me. No more Rio. No more rejection. No more Dane and his monotonous lectures. The rushing water enticed me with its promise of eternal peace. There had to be easier ways to go, admittedly, but the river was here. It was now. If I walked away, I might never find the courage again.

I inched forward, until my bare toes curled over the edge of the jetty. I was so close to sweet oblivion. One more step and it would all be over. *I* would be over. Finally able to sleep without first drinking myself into a stupor. Just one step...

So why wasn't I taking it?

Was there some small part of me that thought this life might be worth living, after all? One tiny spark of hope that was stronger than my desire to end it all.

"Garrison!" Rio's outraged roar sounded from somewhere behind me. "Don't you fucking dare!"

Startled, I spun around to face him. My foot slipped on the wooden planks, still wet and greasy from the heavy rain the day before. Rio's eyes widened and he ran towards me, but he was too late. I was already falling.

I crashed through the surface, icy water closing over my head. Instinctively, I gasped in shock. Dirty river water filled my mouth and lungs, and I couldn't breathe. I fought for the surface, but the current dragged me along and twisted me around until I didn't know which way was up anymore.

Until suddenly, a strange calm came over me. This was what I wanted, wasn't it? I'd had a moment of doubt before fate took the decision out of my hands. My continued existence in this world was not meant to be. Might as well give up the fight and let the river take me. Accept I was dying. It wasn't so bad really. Kind of peaceful once I stopped resisting Death's watery embrace.

I closed my eyes and welcomed the release death would bring.

# Chapter Five

DRIFTING PEACEFULLY AWAY WAS NOT an option in the end. As my head broke the surface of the water, my body automatically began to suck in great, greedy gulps of air. There was a firm body pressed up against my back, a muscled arm locked around my chest. It took me a moment to realize it was Rio. What the fuck was he doing in the water? Didn't he know he could drown?

He kicked his strong legs. Dragging me towards the shore. Disorientated and weak, I wasn't much help. Rio hauled me onto the muddy embankment.

Rio lay on his back, staring up at the sky. I stayed on my hands and knees, puking up the filthy river water I had swallowed. When I was done, I collapsed on the ground beside him. Both of us shivered uncontrollably, as much from shock as from the cold.

Rio saved me and I wasn't even sure how I felt about it. I was going to jump. Then I wasn't. Then I fell anyway, as though it was meant to be. I tried to fight it, but then I thought – *why bother*? I was okay with dying, but then Rio had to go and play the hero and – here we were. Lying in the mud, soaked to the bone, and very probably well on our way to hypothermia.

"Get up," Rio ordered sharply, as he staggered to his feet. "We need to move before we freeze to fucking death."

I took his hand and allowed him to pull me upright. As soon as he was satisfied that I wasn't going to fall straight down again, or throw myself back into the river, he turned away and began the walk back to the cottage.

On shaky legs, I trailed after him. Why was he mad at me? I didn't ask him to jump in and save me. In fact, I wouldn't have fallen in to begin with if he hadn't yelled at me. I mean, shit, if he'd behaved like a decent human being after fucking me senseless, I wouldn't have been out on the jetty in the first place. Everything that just happened was his fault. Not mine.

Thankfully, the current had not carried us as far as I imagined, and we were only two hundred yards from the jetty at most. It was less fortunate that the landscape for the whole two hundred yards consisted of trees and bushes, situated so closely together it was almost impossible to pass between them. Short of going back into the water and swimming against the flow of water, we had no alternative but to battle our way through the trees.

I felt like crying again, as stones and splinters of wood stabbed the soles of my bare feet, but I held the tears in, not wanting to piss Rio off more than he already was.

"Go upstairs and get those wet clothes off," Rio said abruptly, as I limped into the house behind him. "Get into bed and warm up."

"What about you?" I asked, acting uncharacteristically timid. "You're as wet and cold as I am."

"Yeah, well... I'm not the one who just tried to kill myself." He gave me a tired look. "Go on, Garrison. I'll bring you a hot drink up in a minute."

I was tempted to request a medicinal brandy or two but decided I would probably be pushing my luck. Instead, I climbed the narrow staircase with aching limbs and a heavy heart.

Doing as I was told for once in my sorry life, I stripped off the wet clothes and dumped them on the floor of the shower stall. I stole another of Rio's t-shirts from the drawer, before crawling beneath the duvet. I hugged it tight around my frozen body and wondered how long it would take for my teeth to stop chattering.

Rio appeared in the bedroom doorway, bearing mugs of hot, sweet tea. It was good for shock, he told me, setting the mugs down on the bedside cabinet. He took dry clothes into the bathroom to change and emerged wearing a t-shirt and soft sweatpants, which I had forgone in my haste to get beneath the covers.

To my surprise, he climbed into bed beside me and handed me one of the mugs.

"Are you okay?" he asked gruffly.

"I will be once I stop shivering."

"Come here." He put his arm around my shoulders, and I shuffled closer, pressing myself to his side. "Body heat is supposed to help."

"Shouldn't we be naked for that?"

"Take it or leave it." Rio shrugged. "It's a one-time only offer."

"I'll take it then."

As a matter of fact, I felt warmer already, from the weight of his arm around me alone. We sat with our backs to the headboard, sipping our tea and not speaking. Rio's entire body remained rigid, which I took to be mean he was still furious as opposed to cold.

I finished my tea and rested my head on his shoulder with a desolate sigh.

"You hate me, don't you?"

"No, I could never hate you," he replied, his tone flat. "But I am so fucking angry with you right now. I can't even begin to understand why you want to kill yourself. You said you weren't suicidal and then you go and do...*that.*"

"I wasn't going to jump. I mean... I thought about it, but then I changed my mind." My voice was a pathetic whine, even to my own ears. "Falling in was an accident. I didn't jump."

"Thinking about it is bad enough," Rio retorted. "Why do it, Garrison? Because I won't say *I love you*? Is that really worth dying for?"

"No, that's not why!" I said hotly, too ashamed to admit it was at least part of the reason I'd considered ending my own life. "It was a combination of everything. I let shit get on top of me and I shouldn't have. It doesn't matter now, anyway, because I told you... I changed my mind. I don't want to die, Rio."

What I wanted, was to stay in this moment forever. In bed with Rio. His arm around me. A change of conversation would be nice, and it would be even better if he fucked me again. He didn't have to swear his eternal love. Being close to him was enough.

"I saw you," Rio said. "When you were in the water... you didn't fight it. You didn't care if you drowned. You accepted it. So, don't feed me all that bullshit about changing your mind and not wanting to die, because I don't believe you."

A fresh batch of tears burned my eyes. I gripped my empty mug tightly with both hands and didn't bother to wipe them away. They rolled down my face and dripped from my chin onto the duvet. If Rio noticed, he didn't say anything. Not about the tears, at least.

"You need help, Garrison."

"I need you," I whispered softly. "I'm only happy when we're together."

Maybe it was my imagination, but it seemed as though Rio suddenly held me a little tighter. And I definitely must have dreamt the kiss he planted on the top of my head. That would be too much like showing affection for Rio.

"This isn't happening," he said. "It's certainly not love."

I wasn't sure what he meant by that, because who was he to tell me whether I was happy? He had no right to decide if what I felt for him was love or something else. He didn't know what went on in my head or in my heart. It was no wonder I drank. Nothing in my life ever went the way I wanted it to, and it wasn't fair.

"I think I'm warm enough now," I muttered, pulling away from him. I placed the mug on the nightstand and slid down the bed beneath the duvet. I rolled onto my side, turning my back on him.

"Garrison, we need to talk about this."

"You can talk if you like," I answered. "Unless you're cracking open another bottle of your good wine, I'm going back to sleep."

"I'm being serious."

"So am I, and unless the next words out of your mouth are "I want to fuck you, Garrison", I don't want to hear it."

Rio threw back the duvet with a low growl of frustration and got out of bed.

"You're behaving like a child," he said, his anger flaring again.

"Yeah? Well, this *child* needs a nap, so... nighty-night."

"You are fucking impossible!" Rio yelled, losing his cool for once in his life. "You want to know why I don't love you? This is why. There's not a man or woman alive who could put up with you for more than a day."

"If I'm such a terrible person, why didn't you let me drown?"

"Maybe I should have done," Rio snapped. "You know what? If you want to kill yourself so badly, go right ahead. I won't stop you next time."

Through the roaring in my ears, I heard him leave the room. Now the tears flowed thick and fast, and I sobbed, uncontrollably, into the pillow. Fuck. My. Life. I was content to just sit in bed with Rio, but no. As usual, everything had to turn to shit. Rio had said twice now that he didn't hate me, but – not even all that deep down – he must do.

I was a drunk and a loser, but even I knew you didn't tell someone to commit suicide if you liked them even the tiniest, little bit.

# Chapter Six

GOD KNOWS HOW, but I slept the whole day away. Probably, it was because I was too miserable to stay awake. Maybe Rio was right when he said I needed help, because my head was a mess. I wasn't so sure I wanted to die anymore, but nor was I utterly convinced I wanted to live. Things were coming to a head, though, and – one way or the other – I would have to decide and do something about it.

A fistful of Oxy would be a sure-fire way of opting out, so long as I made sure there was nobody around to save me. It almost seemed the easiest option, because living was hard. Living meant sorting myself out, cutting down on my alcohol intake, less screwing around and more proving I could be a reliable, productive member of society. It meant letting go of Rio and moving on. That would be the hardest thing to do, seeing as I was more addicted to him than the booze.

I lay, snuggled beneath the duvet in the darkened room. Motionless. I was in no hurry to go downstairs and face another rejection from Rio. Sooner or later, I would have to, and I knew it was unavoidable, but I could allow myself five more minutes. If I was going to make it through this depression – or whatever the hell was wrong with me – I had to start acting like a grown-up. Pull up my big-boy pants – as Rio so succinctly put it – and face my problems head on.

Problem number one being I was in love with a man who didn't love me back. Problem number two – telling Dane I was having suicidal thoughts. He wouldn't hesitate to help me, but it was painful to admit that I had failed him again.

I heard footsteps on the stairs and then Rio's voice. He stopped in the doorway, from where he could see into the bedroom. How many times had he made the journey upstairs to check on me throughout the day? Maybe it was none at all. It wasn't like he gave a shit.

He spoke softly – presumably on the phone – so as not to wake me.

"He's still asleep. Yeah, I know he's been asleep all day, but he obviously needs it." There was a pause, while the other person spoke. "No, I'm not telling you where we are. There's no point in you coming here anyway. It will only make him worse." Another pause. "I know he's your best friend, but you need to wait until he's ready to talk to you. I'll keep him safe; I promise."

Dane. Who else could it be? He was the only person in my life who gave a damn about me, after all. Even then, it probably had more to do with preserving Jaded Intent than it did me. It was clear from Rio's side of the conversation that Dane knew about the near-drowning incident in the river. No doubt Rio told him it was a suicide attempt, which it really wasn't. At the risk of repeating myself, I didn't jump. I fell. The fact I didn't fight it didn't mean I was trying to kill myself; only that I had surrendered myself to fate.

"Does he hate me?" I asked in a small voice, when Rio ended the call a few minutes later.

"What is it with you and believing everyone hates you?"

Rio came into the room and sat on the side of the bed. He reached over and switched on the lamp, causing me to wince at the sudden brightness.

"How are you feeling?" He looked tired and worried, which was totally my fault.

"Honestly?" I heaved one shoulder in a slight shrug. "I don't know."

"Fair enough." He rested his hand on my hip, and even through the thick duvet, it was like his touch burned my skin. "You said earlier that you don't want to die. Is that the truth?"

"I don't know," I repeated. I dragged my aching body into a seated position so that I was facing him. "If you really want the truth, I haven't made my mind up yet."

Rio frowned. "Meaning?"

"Meaning I've decided how I'll do it, and next time I'll make sure there's nobody around to stop me. But..." I continued quickly, before he could voice his objection, "...I've also decided to talk to Dane, because if anyone can help me through this, it's him."

"What? You don't think I can help you?" Rio asked, scowling.

"No, don't worry. You're off the hook." I flashed him a wry smile. "I love you, Rio. I'm *in* love with you. But I realise loving you isn't good for me." I took a deep breath. "Which is why I'm walking away from you. I can't move on while you're still in my life."

"If that's what you think is best," Rio answered stiffly, looking anything but relieved to be set free from his obligation.

For the life of me, I would never understand this beautiful man. He didn't want me, but then he didn't like it when I said I didn't want him either, like he was jealous of Dane or something. Colour me confused.

"Don't look so disappointed," I said lightly. "I'm sure you'll find someone else to adore you unconditionally."

"That's not why I..." He shook his head and leapt to his feet. "Forget it. Do whatever the fuck you want, just like you always do. I'm going to make you something to eat. Come down when you're ready."

"Rio."

He stopped in the doorway and turned to stare at me.

"If you care so much, why did you leave me?"

His shoulders slumped in defeat. As if he'd waited three years for me to ask the question and now that I had, he couldn't lie to me anymore.

"Because even back then, the drinking and the endless partying was destroying you," he said. "I liked you too much to stick around and watch it happen."

Wait, what? I gaped after him, open-mouthed in surprise, as he made a hasty retreat down the stairs. All this time I thought he left because I told him I loved him. Did he just confess to leaving because *he* loved *me*? Okay, so he said *like* and not *love*, but in this situation, it was tantamount to the same thing. Fuck. I was in deeper shock than when he dragged me from the river.

Rio loved me.

At least, he had back then. I wasn't so sure about now, but... Rio fucking loved me.

He hadn't called the police when I broke into his house. Instead, he'd driven straight down here without telling anyone, even though he knew Dane had the police searching for me. Rio had dived into the freezing river to save me from drowning. He'd taken care of me. Spoken to Dane, even if he chose not to reveal our exact whereabouts. All of that, I would say, meant he still had feelings for me on some level.

With a surprising surge of energy, I jumped out of bed and hurried into the bathroom to empty my bladder and freshen up. I ran my fingers through my tangled hair, which was far from ideal but would have to suffice until I could wash the river water out of it. Back in the bedroom, I borrowed more of Rio's clothes, including socks this time, and made my way downstairs to the kitchen.

Rio was stood at the stove, stirring a jar of Arribiata sauce into a pot of cooked pasta. He glanced up with a hesitant smile when I walked in.

"Lay the table, will you? he said casually and – for a moment – I was afraid what happened upstairs before had been a figment of my fevered imagination.

"Uh... yeah. Sure." I eyed the two-seater table dubiously. "How?"

"What do you mean *how*?" Rio raised his eyebrows. "Are you seriously telling me you've never laid a table before?"

"When I was a kid, maybe," I scoffed. "These days, I eat out of take-away cartons or at restaurants where the tables are already laid."

"I'm sure you'll figure it out," Rio said lightly, trying his best not to sound amused as he pointed to the drawer in which the cutlery was kept.

He observed in silence as I took two glasses from the cupboard and filled them with orange juice. It wasn't that I didn't want an alcohol beverage - I pretty much *always* wanted one – but I was determined to prove I could go without. Rio was better than booze any day of the week. And, yes, I had promised myself I would walk away from him, but that was before he confessed to caring about me.

"I would have stopped," I blurted out as soon as we were both sat at the table with heaped bowls of steaming pasta in front of us. "If you'd said something back then, I would have changed if it meant keeping you."

"The point is, Garrison, you have to want to change for you. Not for me."

"It would have been for me," I argued. "I would have stopped drinking and partying in a heartbeat if you asked me to."

"And then you would have resented me, and we would have broken up anyway."

"Why would I have resented you, when being together was all I ever wanted?" I questioned. "I'm not an alcoholic, whatever everybody thinks. I drink because I want to, not because I need to. It helps me forget how bloody miserable and lonely I am most of the time. And guess what? If you hadn't run out on me the moment I told you I loved you, I wouldn't be either of those things."

"We wouldn't have worked." Rio sighed and stared morosely into his rapidly cooling pasta. "Long distance relationships never do. Once I went back to Carnival, we would hardly have seen each other. Fuck, half the time we're on separate continents. If Carnival isn't touring, then Jaded Intent is and vice versa. There are too many temptations on the road. You know there is. Booze. Drugs. Other people. That goes double for you, when you fuck both men and women."

"I would never have cheated on you," I said hotly. Rio shrugged and shovelled a forkful of pasta into his mouth to avoid having to answer. "What you're really saying is, you wouldn't have been faithful to me."

"I wouldn't cheat. Not if we were together. I..." He shot me an awkward look across the table. "I couldn't trust you. It would have driven me crazy, being apart from you and never knowing if you were with someone else."

"That's not fair! You didn't even give us a chance because of something you thought I might do."

"No, that's not it," Rio answered with another sigh. "I didn't trust you, because you'd already proved to me that I couldn't."

"How did I do that?" I demanded, angry that he was making excuses and trying to blame me for his failure to commit.

"You really don't know?"

"Would I be asking if I did?"

"Fine. I'll tell you. I can't trust you because when I came looking for you at the Wembley after-party, I found you on your knees, sucking off some random guy in the bathroom."

"Oh, piss off!" I retorted scornfully. "I think I'd remember if that happened."

"Yeah, I thought so too," Rio told me. "Seeing as – after you finished blowing him – you decided to announce to the entire room that you loved me."

# Chapter Seven

THERE WAS nothing much I could say to that. I had no defence, other being drunk and probably high, which kind of proved Rio's point. I was a drunk and I cheated on him when I was supposed to be in love with him. All along, I thought Rio was the bastard for breaking my heart, never realising I had broken his first. I didn't remember being with anyone else that night – I barely remembered doing the show – but I believed Rio when he said it happened.

Saying sorry felt like too little too late. How could I even begin to make up for something that happened years ago? Especially as I had no memory of doing anything wrong and I'd only just found out anything happened in the first place.

So, we ate in subdued silence and when we were finished, Rio cleared the plates away. He dropped them into the sink and turned back to face me.

"Call Dane," he said, handing me his phone.

"Is it okay if I take it outside?"

It was dark and cold out there, but if I was going to talk to Dane, I wanted it to be in private. I had to know if he'd been aware all along the real reason for Rio dumping me. And if he did know, why the fuck had he never said anything?

"Stay where I can see you," Rio said sharply.

I nodded. I guess I couldn't blame him for not wanting me out of sight after my little escapade in the river.

Standing just outside the open back door, I found Dane's number and tapped the call button. Dane answered on the first ring, as though he had his phone in his hand and was sat waiting for it to ring.

"Talk to me, Rio," he barked by way of greeting.

"It's me," I said.

I heard Dane suck in a sharp breath before he spoke again.

"Do you have any idea how pissed off I am with you? Only, after today, I can't even say it, can I, in case you try to kill yourself again. I mean, jumping in the fucking river? What the hell were you thinking?"

"I wasn't thinking," I sighed. "And I didn't jump. I slipped."

"That's not what Rio says."

"Yeah, well... who are you going to believe? Your best friend of fuck knows how many years, or the guy who fucked me and then told me he doesn't want me, when he knows I'm supposedly suicidal?"

Dane groaned. "You slept with Rio."

"Actually, yes, but that part came later. First, we fucked. Then I fell in the river – totally Rio's fault, by the way – *then* we slept together in the same bed."

Standing in the open doorway, Rio rolled his eyes and glared. Whatever. Listening to my private conversation was his choice. He only had himself to blame if he didn't like what he heard.

"Well, I assume from your shitty attitude that you're okay," Dane said stiffly. "So, what next, Garrison? Where do we go from here?"

"Honestly, I don't know. I'm a mess, Dane, but I don't want to die. I just... I'm not ready to come back. I think I need to be alone for a while."

"Alone with Rio, you mean." I could imagine Dane scowling on the other end of the phone. "It's not a good idea. You and Rio are never going to work. All you ever do is hurt each other."

"Maybe it will be different this time."

"And maybe it won't. Look, I love Rio, but I love you more. Being with Rio is only ever going to end badly."

"It's not your choice," I said. No, it was Rio's and he'd already made it clear he didn't want a relationship. "You need to give me some space, Dane. Keep pushing me and I'll walk away. From you. The band. Everything."

I hung up and handed the phone back to Rio. He leaned against the door frame, regarding me solemnly through hooded eyes.

"No," he said.

"I haven't asked you anything."

"I can't be your happiness, Garrison."

"I'm not asking you to be!"

"It kind of feels like you are."

He pushed away from the door frame and went back into the cottage. I followed him, annoyed. I wasn't asking him to be responsible for my happiness. Whatever the fuck that meant. Despite what I said to Dane, I knew Rio and I were not good for each other. I thought it had already been agreed in the bedroom that we would be going our separate ways.

"You're replacing me with alcohol," Rio said, "and it's not going to work."

"Bullshit!" I snapped. "That's not what I'm doing. I'm finally trying to sort my life out and you've made it clear you don't want to be a part of it. It's fine, Rio. I get it. No hard feelings, eh?"

"Fuck, Garrison, I *always* have hard feelings when it comes to you." He grabbed my hand and pulled me close to his body, turning my world upside down with the flick of a split personality switch. "Go to bed with me."

I snorted, not caring that I never knew where I stood with him.

"Like you have to ask."

*Chapter Eight*

WAKING UP, limbs my entangled with Rio's, was the best feeling. Last night with Rio was different to any other time we'd had sex before. Rio was uncharacteristically gentle and caring. It felt like he was making love. Talk about sending mixed messages.

Shifting as carefully as I could, I tilted my head back to study Rio's face. He was still asleep, his lashes long and dark against his lightly tanned skin. I took my time, studying his handsome face, his lightly tanned skin and perfectly shaped lips that hid straight white teeth. The man really was a walking-talking wet dream.

"Didn't anyone ever tell you it's rude to stare?" Rio said, those luscious lips curving into a faint smile.

"Yeah, but I don't think it applies when you're in bed with the hottest guy on the planet."

Rio chuckled and opened his eyes. "Sweet talk will get you everywhere." He stretched lazily. "What do you want to do today?"

"Stay in bed and fuck our brains out." I didn't need to think about my answer. No lifelines necessary. No ask the audience or fifty/fifty, and even if I did call a friend, there was only Dane, and he would tell me not to do it.

"Didn't you get enough last night?"

"Of you?" I shook my head. "Never."

Was that too much too soon? So, we slept together again. It didn't necessarily mean anything. It didn't mean Rio had suddenly changed his mind about being with me in the long term, any more than it changed mine about not wanting to be with him. I was not going to lie to myself and deny that I was still in love with him, but – at the same time – I needed to face up to the fact Rio was not good for my mental health in the long run.

"I was thinking more along the lines of going into town and getting you a few bits and pieces," Rio said dryly. "A change of clothes, perhaps, and a toothbrush so you stop using mine all the damn time."

I rested my chin on his chest and stared up at him.

"That would imply I'm staying here."

"Yeah, well... a couple of days won't hurt, will it?" Rio gave a casual shrug. "Then I have to go back to London anyway, and you can go back to Dane."

A couple of days and then we went our separate ways. Forty-eight hours to pretend we were a couple and simply enjoy each other's company. I guess I was okay with that. I wasn't so sure about leaving the cottage, though. Not when the whole point of being here was to escape life in the public eye.

"What if we're recognised?"

"What if we are?"

"I don't know. I would rather *not* be, that's all." I rolled off him and sat up. "I think I'm going to stop dying my hair. I'm going to cut it too."

"Okay, if you sure you want to. But isn't your black hair like a trademark look?" Rio eyed me dubiously. "The fans won't like it if you change your appearance too much. No doubt Dane will have something to say about it too."

"I'm thirty-four," I argued, "and I've had the same hairstyle since I was eighteen. I think I'm due a change. Besides, the fans won't see it. Not if I leave Jaded Intent."

Rio sat up. "You wouldn't."

"Not straight away, maybe." I was thinking on my feet, but suddenly the future seemed so much clearer. I hadn't figured out the finer details yet, but this was what I wanted. "I'll do the studio album, but I'm going on tour again."

"Could you really give it up though?" Rio asked. "You would miss being on the road too much."

"I doubt it, but if it happens, I'll have to become your number one groupie and go on tour with you," I said lightly. "Seriously, Rio, it's better I walk away from the limelight now than end up dead in the not-too-distant future."

"Fuck, Dane is going to kill me." Rio swung his legs out of bed and sat on the edge of the mattress. "If you leave, he'll blame me."

"He won't. He'll understand. I mean, obviously he won't want me to leave the band, but he won't want me dead either. At least, I hope he doesn't," I added thoughtfully.

After the way I'd behaved, especially over the last year, I wouldn't blame him if he wanted rid of me. Since playing that nightmare gig with Rio for Dane's cousin, CJ, I'd spiralled out of control. I knew that. But things came to a head when I unintentionally tried to kill myself and now, I was thinking straight for the first time in ages. I knew what needed to be done if I wanted to live to be thirty-five.

"Maybe you should call him before you do anything drastic like cutting your hair or quitting the band," Rio suggested in all seriousness.

I stared at his back in disbelief for a second or two, before shoving his shoulder.

"Running away and coming here was drastic," I scoffed. "Breaking into your house was drastic. Falling in the river and almost drowning was most definitely drastic. Cutting my hair? Not so much. I'm a grown fucking man. I don't need Dane's permission."

"Yeah, not sure Dane will see it the same way," Rio muttered.

He stood up and stretched. My eyes went instantly to the taut muscles of his arse, and I had to forcibly restrain myself from reaching over and grabbing a nice, meaty handful. Personally, I was very much in favour of staying in bed and fucking each other senseless. Forty-eight hours and it would all be over. I needed to get my fill of him while I had the chance, because all too soon he would be gone again.

I rolled out of bed with a sigh. Evidently, Rio was not willing to play ball. Or – more to the point – play with *my* balls. Maybe if I was a good boy while we were out, I would be suitably rewarded later. My own clothes were clean and folded on a chair. Apparently, Rio washed and dried them while I slept yesterday. Who knew he was a domestic goddess as well as drop-dead-fucking-gorgeous?

"Are we taking your car?" I asked as I got dressed.

"No, it will attract too much attention," Rio answered. "There's a guy in the village who operates a taxi service into town. I'll give him a call."

"I thought you didn't care if we're recognised?"

"I don't, but it doesn't mean we have to advertise the fact we're in town. Someone is bound to put it on Facebook or Instagram. Do you want Dane to know where you are?"

He was right, of course. As much as I would have liked a quick spin in the Stingray, I didn't want it to be at the cost of Dane finding out my location. He would be in Devon in a matter of hours and track me down by nightfall. There were probably plenty of locals who knew Rio Darke had a cottage on the bank of the Dart. They might shield the exact whereabouts from the press, but I bet they would tell Dane Black if he asked nicely. I didn't want him showing up and thinking he could drag me back to London and stick me into rehab again. For the sake of my sanity, I needed this time with Rio.

Thankfully, when we were dropped off in the nearest town, nobody really paid us much attention. It helped that we had woollen beanie hats pulled down over our ears. Plus, I was basically dressed like a tramp, even if my clothes were freshly laundered. Naturally, Rio still managed to look like a walking wet dream and people – men, women, young and old – shot him coy looks as he passed. It didn't matter if they knew who he was or not. The man was as hot as fuck.

Nobody bothered us though, as we wandered in and out of different shops, purchasing the few bits and pieces I needed to tide me over for the next couple of days. We ate lunch in a small café, where – for the first time – there was a notable buzz of excitement among the other patrons, some of whom clearly recognised us. A couple dared to approach us once we finished eating and we spent the next half hour signing napkins and posing for photos. Dane would soon know we were in Devon once the pictures were posted on social media, but he wouldn't know where.

After, when we politely managed to make our escape, I spied a barber shop on the other side of the road and dragged Rio over to the door. Luckily, there were no customers, so I slipped inside, and Rio followed, albeit with reservation written clearly on his face. It was obviously a slow day for business, because I could only see one guy, bored out of his skull and spinning in circles on a stool.

It was just our luck he was a massive fan of Carnival and of Rio in particular. He stopped spinning so abruptly that he almost fell off the stool.

"Holy fuck, you're Rio Darke! In my shop. Rio Darke is in my shop. Holy fuck!" he gabbled in excitement. He jumped up from the stool as if he was going to rush over and hug Rio. Instead, he held up his hands defensively and backed away. "No way am I cutting your hair, man. I'm not worthy."

"Not mine," Rio agreed. He whipped the beanie from my head before I could stop him. "His."

"Holy... Garrison! Shit, I must be dreaming." He squeezed his eyes shut. When he opened them again, it was hard to tell if he was relieved to find we were real. "What are you two doing together? Aren't you supposed to be like rivals or something?"

"Let's just say, if we were on Facebook, our relationship status would come under complicated," Rio replied, laughing. "So, can you give him a trim or not?"

"Sure, I'd be happy to do it."

It was nice to know he felt worthy enough to cut my hair. Obviously, he didn't idolise me as much as he did Rio. I wasn't bothered. That kind of adoration from strangers never sat easy with me. It was one of the things I was hoping to escape by leaving Jaded Intent.

The kid – Dwyane, as he introduced himself while he was leading me to a chair – baulked a little when I told him what I wanted. Then he got on with the job and I closed my eyes, not wanting to see until it was finished, and silently praying I didn't hate it. While Dwyane worked, he chatted comfortably with Rio. He didn't seem to notice Rio had positioned himself in front of the door and turned the sign to 'closed', so nobody else could come in. Whether it was for his sake or mine was open to debate, but I liked to think he did it for me. Not just because it was further proof that he cared, but because it showed he understood the enormity of what was happening. Cutting my hair was symbolic. It was the first step on the road to my new life.

"There. Done," Dwayne said after what felt like an absolute age had passed. "It suits you, man."

Still, I hesitated to open my eyes, afraid I wouldn't recognise the man in the mirror. Strong hands landed on my shoulders. Without thinking I reached up and grasped them. Which was going to be pretty fucking embarrassing if it wasn't Rio.

Cautiously, I opened my eyes, but it was Rio's reflection I focused on rather than my own. He smiled.

"Regretting it?"

"No, I..." I swallowed nervously. "Should I be? Is it awful? Do you hate it?"

"That would be no, no and no," Rio said, amused. "Look for yourself, beautiful. Dwayne did a good job."

Talking of Dwayne, had Rio forgotten the kid was standing two feet away? What was he doing, bandying about casual terms of endearment in front of people? It wasn't true anyway. I mean, I was okay-looking, but I wasn't beautiful like Rio. Without my long, black hair I wasn't sure people would even consider me to be okay either.

I took a deep breath and slowly lowered my gaze. Well... it wasn't horrific. It was still me still the same hazel eyes staring back, although they seemed lighter somehow. Less troubled, as if a weight had lifted from my heart as well as my head. I looked older, but not old. More mature, maybe. More my real age as opposed to a man trying to look like he was still in his twenties. The style was short enough that most of the black dye had been cut away and what remained was my natural mousy brown.

Rio lifted his hands to card his fingers through the short strands.

"I love it," he said softly.

I met his eyes in the mirror.

"I love *you.*"

He dropped his hands to his sides and took a step back.

"You need to pay the man," he said, his tone suddenly brusque. "I'll wait for you outside."

# Chapter Nine

I SHOULDN'T HAVE SAID it. Rio had been quiet and brooding ever since, which made for an uncomfortable taxi ride back to the cottage. He knew I meant it and therein lay the problem. He didn't want to take responsibility for me, I got that, but he was giving off all kinds of mixed signals.

I didn't mean the sex. Both of us were living proof that sex was just sex at the end of the day, regardless of who it was with. But the other stuff – asking me to stay, the way I caught him looking at me at times, and countless little touches – all of that told me he cared. It was more than helping a friend, but Rio was not prepared to commit because he didn't trust me not to hurt him again.

When we got back to the cottage, I took my bags upstairs and unpacked. This time tomorrow, I would be packing them up again to go to Dane's house, but for now, it was nice to put my stuff into a drawer next to Rio's and pretend it was forever. Going downstairs, I found Rio out on the patio, talking animatedly into his phone. The conversation didn't appear to be about me for once, so I left him to it. I guess he pulled his own disappearing act when he came to rescue me just weeks before his tour started, so he probably had his own repercussions to deal with. Carnival's lead singer, Cage, was not known for his easy-going nature at the best of times.

I walked back through the house and out of the front door. It was cold, down on the riverbank, but I sat on the grass and hugged my knees to my chest to try and preserve what small amount of body warmth I had. At least it wasn't raining, although an icy wind blew in from the water, making me shiver. In a way, I quite liked it. *Let it blow the cobwebs away,* that's what my old gran used to say, and even though I was the best I had been in a long time, I could still do with clearing my head.

"If you're thinking of jumping in, don't expect me to save you this time."

Rio startled me, because I didn't hear him coming. It was a good job I wasn't stood at the end of the dock, or I might well have fallen in again. I had no clue how long I had been sat there, but from the stiffness in my bones suggested it was longer than a few minutes.

"Don't worry." I tilted my head back to smile up at him. "Once was enough."

"What are you doing out here? Aren't you cold?"

"A little bit," I lied. More like freezing my nuts off, but I didn't want him fussing over me. "I'm enjoying watching the river and the birds, though, and the occasional boat go by. It's peaceful. My mind is peaceful."

Actually, I hadn't been doing any of those things, and my mind wasn't peaceful so much as empty. Completely devoid of any thought whatsoever. Which, knowing the way my mind worked, wasn't necessarily a bad thing.

Rio sighed and sat on the grass beside me.

"I wish I could leave you here when I go back to London, but..."

"But you don't trust me not to try and kill myself the second I'm on my own. You're probably right not to. I'm not sure I trust myself either."

Rio frowned. "You said you didn't want to die."

"I don't. Today. I can't promise how I'm going to feel about it after you leave."

"Garrison..." He sighed again and rubbed his hands over his face.

"Don't do this to me. I told you before, I can't be responsible for your happiness."

"I know, but I'm trying to be honest with you. It's like you ground me, Rio. I can't go back to my old life and be the way I was before, but without you, I don't know how long I can resist. Then it's only a matter of time before I'm right back where I started and offing myself feels like the only way out of a life I don't want. That's not the person I want to be anymore."

Rio stared at me intently for a long, long moment. He was probably trying to decide if he believed me, when I was being the most truthful with him that I had ever been. Apart from the bit about not being cold. I was fucking freezing.

"Come back to London with me," he blurted out breathlessly.

"I thought I already was," I said, bemused. "Aren't you handing babysitting duty over to Dane?"

"No, I mean... move in with me."

"Rio..." I shook my head. "That's not why I'm saying any of this."

"I'm serious. It only gives us a month before I have leave for the North America tour, but maybe we can use the time to try and figure out all this shit between us."

"I don't understand. Why would you even want to?" I asked.

Two days and then it was all over. That was what we agreed. I thought it was what Rio wanted. He wrapped his arm around my shoulders, and I leaned against him, trying to suppress my shivers.

"You know why," he said quietly, even though there was nobody around to hear him but for me and a couple of cormorants.

"I don't know for sure unless you say it."

Yet more of the truth. I didn't know where I stood with him from one minute to the next. If I so much as mentioned the word love, he backed off faster than a Ferrari. At the same time, he showed me repeatedly that he was reluctant to let me go. There had to be more to it than him not wanting to bear the weight of the guilt if anything happened to me.

"We should go back inside," he said gruffly, getting to his feet. "We need to get you thawed out."

"In bed?" I asked hopefully, taking his proffered hand and letting him pull mc to my feet.

"You, maybe. I'll bring you up a hot drink, but then I've got some phone calls to make."

"Should I be jealous?"

"Not of Cage, no." I shot him a questioning look and he responded with a wry smile. "You're not the only one whose bandmates are wondering where the fuck you disappeared to."

"Do they know about this place?"

"Hell, no," Rio retorted. "I come here to get away from them. If Cage knew it existed, he'd expect to use it as his own, personal knocking-shop. Don't ask," he added, when I raised my eyebrows.

It was only a matter of months since Carnival's lead singer was released from prison after doing time for assault. Obviously, he hadn't learned anything. Cage might think twice about beating up the next photographer who snapped him cheating on his wife, but obviously he had no intention of not cheating in the first place.

Once inside, I didn't really mind being sent to bed to warm up. I took my boots off and crawled beneath the duvet, fully clothed. I decided I may as well call Dane while I waited for Rio to bring me hot drink up. I owed him an apology for the way I ended the call the night before. Depending on how he took it, I would consider telling him I was moving in with Rio.

I realised I hadn't given Rio a definite answer yet, but... come on. I was hardly going to say no, was I?

Dane answered on the first ring. I could imagine him, pacing around his house with his phone in his hand all day, waiting for me to call. He'd probably argued with Riley over whether he should call me first. He sounded relieved to hear from me, which made me wish I was a better friend to him. The man had my back. Always.

"Sorry," I said. "I was acting like a prick last night."

"Yeah, well, I'm sorry too." It was typical Dane, answering an apology with an apology of his own. I didn't even deserve one after all the crap I'd put him through in recent months. If I was totally honest, my behaviour had been appalling for years, but it was only since seeing Rio again at CJ's gig that I'd allowed it to get completely out of control.

"It's not my place to choose your relationships for you," Dane continued, "but I love you like a brother, Garrison. If anything happened to you…"

"It won't," I said, although I knew it would take a lot more than words to reassure him. He would only be fully satisfied once he could see me with his own eyes and had me back under his protection. Because yeah – that had worked wonders so far. *Not.* "Listen, I know I went about it the wrong way, but being here has been really good for me. I'm sober. I'm eating properly. My head feels like it's on straight for the first time on forever."

"I still don't know where *here* is," Dane complained. "Rio won't tell me."

"Neither will I. Trust me, Rio has his reasons for keeping this place a secret."

"Fine, then I guess I need to respect that. You sound happy. I take it things are going well between you."

"Yeah, we're cool. We've still got shit to sort out…" Like Rio's basic inability to admit he was in love with me. "…but we're getting there."

There was a long pause on the other end of the phone. I knew Dane thought I was kidding myself. That Rio was stringing me along and I was going to end up getting hurt again.

"He asked me to move in with him." God, could I sound anymore defensive? "Only for a month until he goes on tour."

"And what happens when he leaves?" Dane asked stiffly. Shit. He hated the idea, but then I knew that he would. "What happens when he breaks your heart again?"

"Well, then I guess you get to do what you do best, which is pick up the pieces and say I-told-you-so."

"I'd rather it didn't get to that stage," Dane said. "Which it won't, if you just end this now."

"You want me to stop?" I leaned back against the pillows and closed my eyes. "Then tell me how, Dane. Tell me how to stop loving him, because God knows I would if I could."

Opening my eyes again, I saw Rio framed in the bedroom doorway, a steaming mug clutched in his right hand. He set the mug down on top of the chest of drawers.

"I brought you a hot chocolate," he said.
Then he turned and went back down the stairs.

<h1 style="text-align:center">Chapter Ten</h1>

RIO'S RENTED townhouse was one hundred times nicer than the modern apartment I'd bought a few years ago. His home was warm and inviting, whereas mine was cold and lonely and not much of a home at all. It was no wonder I hardly spent any time there, preferring to stay at Dane's, or with whoever would have me for the night. I didn't even keep any food in the big, American-style fridge as I always ate out or ordered in.

If I was genuinely going to make the effort to change my life, selling the place was high on my list of priorities. It didn't make me happy, therefore it had to go. I would stay with Dane while we worked on the studio album and then I would buy myself a small cottage by the sea.

Not that I'd told Dane I was leaving Jaded Intent yet. That was a conversation we needed to have face to face. Rio mentioned inviting Dane and Riley over for dinner one evening soon, so maybe I would do it then. Or maybe not. Dane was going to blame Rio for me quitting the band and if he did, it would be better if Rio was not around at the time.

I was surprised, quite frankly, when Rio still wanted me to stay with him. He denied it, of course, but I knew I'd injured his feelings when I said I would stop loving him if I could. I didn't know for sure, because he refused to discuss it. True to character, he sulked for a while and then carried on as if nothing had happened. Not for the first time, he backed away from me while objecting to the idea I wanted to back off from him. I loved him, but... man, he was infuriating at times.

"Which room am I in?" I asked, as Rio gave me the grand tour of the three-storey house.

There were two guest bedrooms, a full-size bathroom and a games room on the top floor, while Rio's master bedroom was on the middle floor, along with a lounge and a huge, modern bathroom with a rainforest shower head.

"Mine, obviously," Rio replied, rolling his eyes as if to say it was not only a stupid question but one to which I should have known the answer.

And maybe I should have done, because he asked me to move him with him. Move in. With him. Not as a housemate or a lodger but as a partner. A lover. I tried not to get too excited, reminding myself this was only a temporary arrangement as I unpacked my meagre belongings into the drawer he'd emptied for me.

"We can swing by your place later and pick up some of your stuff," Rio offered.

"Thanks, but a lot of it is at Dane's house," I admitted, only now realising that I had been in the slow process of moving out of my apartment for months. If Dane had registered the fact I basically lived in his home these days; he didn't say anything. "I know he's got my guitar in his music room."

"Do you want to go over and grab what you want, or shall we ask Dane to bring it here?"

"I don't know. I suppose if we ask Dane to come here, he can bring Riley and we can have dinner together. I mean, we were going to invite them anyway, weren't we?"

"If you're sure you're ready to face him," Rio said from his reclined position on the king-sized bed, from where he had watched me put my clothes away. "Are you going to tell him you're leaving Jaded Intent?"

"Maybe. I'll see what mood he's in first. I know it's only fair to tell him, but if he's going to be a dick about it and blame you..."

"I'm a big boy," Rio laughed. "I can take it."

"Well, how is that fair?" I teased, changing the mood by stalking across the bedroom with a predatory smile. "When you won't take me."

Rio narrowed his eyes, his luscious lips curling upwards.

"Baby, I *take* you all the time," he taunted.

"Not inside you."

I climbed onto the bed and straddled his thighs. My fingers reached for the button on his jeans.

Rio caught hold of my wrists.

"There's a reason for that, sweetheart. I don't bottom."

"Oh, but I promise to be gentle with you." I pulled free of his grasp and grabbed for his fly again. "And stop with the pet names. It's tacky, especially when you don't even mean it."

Rio lunged, seizing me around the waist and rolling us over so that he was the one on top. I could easily flip us back if I tried, but why would I want to? I knew he would never agree to bottom for me, but he'd fallen into my trap and now I had him right where I wanted him. Well... almost. I could think of better places for his erection to be poking me than in my thigh.

"Who says I don't mean it?" his blue-eyed gaze burning into my soul.

"You do," I said sadly, "every time I tell you I love you and you walk away from me."

His response was to kiss me. It was a kiss filled with longing and desire. A kiss that told me all the things Rio couldn't put into words. It washed away my fear and doubt and replaced them with unadulterated love.

Without breaking our lips apart, we groped blindly at our respective buttons and zips, awkwardly shoving our jeans down as far as it took to free our cocks. Rio shifted his weight until our dicks were lined up, all the while kissing me like it was going out of fashion. We rutted together, desperate and horny, like teenagers going at it for the first time. Hands grabbed. Teeth and lips clashed.

It was fast. It was dirty.

It was hot as hell, and I loved every second.

## Chapter Eleven

DANE ARRIVED with Riley in tow, a little after six. I helped them lug my bags and guitars into the house. We left them in the hallway for Rio and me to carry upstairs later, mainly because Riley had a face on him like a slapped arse and I didn't dare impose on him further. Never my biggest fan in the first place, he was probably put out enough at having to spend an entire evening in my company. He hated it whenever he thought Dane was putting my needs before his. It made me think back to a few days ago, when he'd refused to let me speak to Dane and then hung up on me. I bet he never even told Dane that I called. Then again, if he had, I might not have ended up in Rio's bed, so I ought to be thanking him for resenting my existence as much as he did.

Although, him not telling Dane about the call probably explained why he was being so pissy with me now. He was scared I would let it slip and get him into trouble with his boyfriend. If he didn't wind his neck in, I would bring it up accidently on purpose.

"What the fuck have you done to your hair?" Dane asked, ignoring Riley's bad mood and turning to give me a hard stare instead. "You look ridiculous. Oh, well, I suppose it will grow back."

I pulled a face and didn't answer. Me leaving the band was not a conversation I wanted to have out in the hallway.

I needn't have worried about causing tension, though, because it didn't take long, though, to figure out Riley was as pissed off with Dane as he was with me and that was out of character. Usually, Riley thought the sun shone out of Dane's backside. I hoped I wasn't the reason they were fighting. They were good together. I might not care for Riley that much, but Dane did. I would have to try harder to get along with the little twink, because I genuinely didn't want to come between them.

Rio ordered enough Chinese food to feed a small army and we all sat around a large, highly polished table in the ground floor dining room. Music played softly in the background, the muted melody and lyrics too serene to belong to either Jaded Intent or Carnival.

"I didn't have you down for a romance kind of guy," Dane remarked, heaping a mountain of food onto his plate.

I'd probably eaten more in this past couple of days with Rio than I had in months, but – despite the return of my appetite – I was still no match for Dane's bottomless pit of a stomach.

"I have my moments," Rio answered dryly. "Just ask Garrison."

"Not me," I scoffed, popping a piece of salt-and-pepper chicken into my mouth. "You must be thinking of one of the many, *many* others you've been with."

"There haven't been that many!" Rio protested, a cute blush turning his cheeks pink. "Just the odd one here and there to pass the time."

"Hundreds," I teased in a dramatic stage whisper. "Maybe even thousands. Am I right?"

"No, you're wrong," Rio shook his head and grinned at me.

"Yeah, Garrison," Riley chimed in, apparently oblivious to the game Rio and I were playing. "Not everyone is a total slut like you."

"Riley!" Dane said sharply.

"What? It's true, isn't it?" Riley snapped, defensive and unrepentant.

"Hold on," I said in annoyance. "Rio has slept with just as many people as I have."

"Oh, please..." Riley retorted, his voice heavy with scorn and derision. "*Nobody* has slept with as many people as you have."

"What the fuck, Riley?" Dane demanded. "You're a guest in this house, so start acting like one. Don't take it out on Garrison because you're mad at me."

"Don't defend him all the time!" Riley pushed his chair back from the table and leapt to his feet. "You never put me first and I'm sick of it!"

He turned and ran from the room. A few moments later, we heard the front slam. Dane shrugged and carried on eating like nothing his boyfriend ditching him was no big deal. For once, I had a feeling whatever Riley's temper tantrum was about, it had little to do with me.

"Trouble in paradise?" I asked lightly.

Dane fixed me with a steely-eyed stare across the table.

"Sorry, I wasn't being flippant," I said, hoping he could hear the sincerity in my voice. I didn't know how to do this supportive kind of shit. It was Dane's job to drag me out of the gutter. It was never the other way around. "You're my best friend, Dane. You know you can talk to me, right?"

"Actually, no, I don't," Dane replied. "It's not entirely your fault either. I mean, yeah, I always figure you've got too much shit of your own going on to bother you with mine, but – having said that – I don't really have any major problems, anyway. Other than you disappearing on me, of course."

"Looks like you've got one now," Rio said, nodding to the door Riley had just left by. "What did you do? Forget your anniversary?"

"I wish it was that simple." Dane sighed. "But if you must know, I've been slapped with a bullshit paternity suit, and, needless to say, Riley is none too pleased about it."

"Wait, when did that happen?"

"Just this morning," Dane said.

I gaped at him stupidly. "You had sex with a woman this morning?"

"No, you idiot. The letter telling me she's suing for paternity arrived this morning." Dane rolled his eyes. "I'm a gold star gay and you know it. I've never been near a vagina in my life. I was even born by caesarean."

Rio laughed. "Now that's dedication."

"I know, right?" Dane grinned and carried on eating. Nothing came between him and his food, even boyfriend trouble. If I was upset, anxious or ill, my body went into automatic starvation mode. Not so with Dane. "Anyway, I don't know this woman. To the best of my knowledge, I've never met her. God knows why she picked me to be her baby-daddy."

"Could it have been CJ?" Rio asked, naming Dane's cousin. "You guys look so alike you could be twins."

"We're not *that* similar," Dane argued around a mouthful of egg-fried rice. "CJ wouldn't do that to me, anyway. He wouldn't cheat on Boone, and if he did, it wouldn't be with a woman. He's strictly a dick guy, same as me."

"So, what are you going to do about it?"

It was a miracle nobody had ever come after me. Other than the woman I'd woken up next to a few days ago, my sexual partners had been exclusively male in the three years since Rio dumped me. It wasn't always that way, though. I'd bedded more than my fair share of women in my time and hadn't always been careful. There were plenty of times in the past when I'd been too drunk or too high to care about using protection. If there were any mini-Garrisons running around out there, I didn't know about them. It was probably for the best. No kid deserved a fuck-up like me for a dad.

"It will sort itself out," Dane said, unconcerned. "A simple DNA test will prove I'm not the father."

"Why is Riley taking it so badly?" That was Rio. I couldn't give a toss about how Riley was taking it, other than for the fact he was acting like a total dickwad towards Dane. "Doesn't he believe you?"

"He believes me," Dane answered, "but he's been hurt badly in the past and all this is dragging up some painful memories. Added to you going AWOL and worrying the shit out me, Riley's feeling a little insecure at the moment."

"Shouldn't you go after him?"

Rio again. I wasn't sure I was happy with him showing so much concern for Riley. Somehow, it cheapened everything he was doing for me. It didn't have the same meaning if he would do the same thing for any Tom, Dick and Harry. And, yes, I was being a jealous fuck, but I didn't want to be just another name on his long list of charitable deeds. I wanted to be special. To know he was with me because he loved me and not out of pity.

"Riley will be fine," Dane said, helping himself to another over-sized portion of Szechuan Pork. Seriously, the guy should be the size of a house with everything he ate. Which he pretty much was, but it was all muscle. Dane didn't have an ounce of fat on his body. "He'll sit on the doorstep and cry for a bit, then he'll come back in."

Sure enough, not even five minutes later, the doorbell rang. I was first to my feet.

"I'll get it."

From the faces they made, I could tell that neither Dane nor Rio were particularly keen on the idea, but I was already on my way out of the room. They were probably afraid I'd refuse to allow Riley back into the house. It was no secret we didn't like each other. Dane and Rio were right to worry. I'd make my decision on whether I let him in or not, based on his reaction to it being me opened the door. If he was a dick about it, I'd slam the door in his face and not even feel guilty about it. Only when I opened the door, that face was red and blotchy from crying. He looked young and kind of pathetic, and I felt sorry for him. A little bit at least. I still thought he was a prick.

"Can I come in?" he asked stiffly, not meeting my gaze.

"Sure." I stepped back to allow him into the hallway. "He wouldn't cheat on you, you know. Especially not with a woman."

"I know," Riley sniffled.

If he started crying again, I'd chuck him straight back through the front door I hadn't got around to closing yet. I couldn't deal with tears.

"It's just so hard," he continued. "It's never ever just me and him. There's you, always hanging around, taking up his time and attention. And if it's not you, it's Dozer or KP, or the rest of the fucking world, because he's Dane Black and everybody wants a piece of him. He'll never really be mine, will he?"

I pursed my lips, trying to see this crazy life we lived through the eyes of an outsider. Riley was not part of the music industry. He was not famous. He hadn't even known who Dane was when they first met, therefore, it went without saying he was not a big Jaded Intent fan. Poor guy had no idea in the beginning, that dating a rock-star meant sharing him with Joe Public every minute of every day. I would have thought it would get easier with time, but obviously that wasn't true in Riley's case. Now, some psycho-bitch claiming Dane was the father of her child, seemed to be the straw that broke the camel's back. I sighed, and pushed the door shut.

"Dane loves you more than anything," I told him truthfully. "I've known him a long time, and he's never loved anyone the way he does you."

"Not even you?" Riley asked bitterly.

"He loves me, yeah, but it's not the same. Our love comes from years of friendship. We're brothers at heart, even if not by blood."

Riley gave me a look full of scepticism and doubt.

"So, if Dane asked you to sleep with him, you'd say no?"

"It's a redundant question," I said firmly, "because it's never going to happen. "Dane is in love with you and I'm..."

"You're what?"

"Nothing. Forget it."

"You're in love with Rio. Is that what you were going to say?"

"Yes, but he's not in love with me, so it doesn't really matter, does it?"

"What will you do when he leaves?" Riley asked, sounding like he might actually give a shit.

"I don't know." I shrugged. "Get drunk. Fuck everything with a pulse. Not Dane, of course..." I added quickly. Not anyone else either if I could help it, but I didn't want Riley thinking I'd gone soft. "What do you care?"

"It's like you said, you're Dane's brother. He won't want you to be unhappy or alone. So, if you want to, you can stay with us for as long as you need to."

"I guess I could do that," I answered, like I hadn't been planning on doing it anyway. "Just until I get my own place."

Riley arched an eyebrow. "Don't you already have your own place?"

"Yeah, but I hate it. I'm going to sell it and buy a different place. Maybe a cottage by the sea or something."

"You? In a cottage by the sea? Don't make me laugh." Dane stepped out into the hallway, with Rio behind him. They had obviously been stood in the doorway, listening the whole time. Long enough for Rio to hear me say I was in love with him, because he had that sour look on his face again. The one he got every single time the subject of feelings was broached. "You wouldn't know what to do with yourself," Dane scoffed.

"I'll get by," I argued, suddenly defensive, because – brother or best friend – Dane had no right to shit all over my dreams for the future. "I can write songs and give guitar lessons. Maybe I'll even try writing a book. I've got a whole bunch of ideas."

"Garrison, be serious. What do you know about writing a book? You're a guitarist, not an author. Half the time, you're so drunk you can barely write your own name," Dane said scathingly. It was out of character for him to verbally attack me, and for his tone to be so harsh. He was scared, as if, deep down, he knew what I was building up to and he didn't want to hear it. "And how can you give lessons when you're never going to be there? We've got an album to make, dipshit, and then we're out on tour next year."

"About that..."

I glanced at Rio over Dane's shoulder. He folded his arms and glared back, which was no fucking help whatsoever. How was I supposed to know what that look meant? Was he daring me to tell Dane I was leaving the band? Or was he warning me not to, because it was too soon?

"Don't even fucking think about it!"

Dane looked furious, like he was ready to punch me or Rio – or maybe both of us – in the face. I didn't need to tell him because he already knew. He *fucking knew.* And he was going to blame Rio. Accuse him of putting ideas in my head, because I was incapable of making decisions for myself, right?

"I'll do the album," I said flatly, "but I don't want to go on tour again. Don't go thinking this is Rio's fault either. Leaving the band is my choice, Dane."

Dane shook his head, his eyes ablaze with anger and a large dose of obstinance. I expected him to be angry. What I didn't see coming was his outright refusal to accept what I'd just said.

"I'm not having this conversation," he ground out through gritted teeth. "You need to come home, Garrison. Maybe once you're away from *him*, you'll start thinking a little more clearly."

"Hey, it's nothing to do with me." Rio held up his hands defensively, before retreating to the dining room.

*Yeah, thanks for the support, lover boy.*

"Look at me," I said to Dane. "I mean, really look at me. Can't you see my head is the clearest it's been in a long time? I haven't had a drink in days and I'm thinking straighter than I've ever done."

"You're not seeing sense though, are you?"

"It's exactly what I'm seeing!" I cried in exasperation. "Why can't *you* see that being famous is killing me? I won't survive another tour."

Dane hesitated. He knew every word I said was true. He just didn't want to believe it. His jaw set stubbornly as he pushed past me to front door, Riley chasing after him.

"I can't talk to you when you're like this."

"Like what? Do you mean sober? Would you rather I was drunk? Is that what you're saying?" The pause that came before his weak denial spoke volumes. "Then get the fuck out."

"Don't worry, we're going."

The door slammed behind him and Riley and a moment later I was standing alone in the hallway.

"Well, that went well," I said to nobody at all.

# Chapter Twelve

THE SEX RIO and I had after Dane and Riley had gone, was rushed and hard and angry. It was hate-sex, which resulted in both of us sporting new scratches and bruises and left me with a bite mark on my right shoulder. I didn't mind too much. It was the kind of sex I needed given my bad mood. I didn't understand what Rio had to be pissed off about, though. I mean, okay, Dane blamed him for everything, but we'd known that would be the case from the start. It didn't explain why Rio was mad at me instead of Dane, though. Unless he heard me tell Riley I was in love with him. More often than not, any expression of sentiment was enough to send him into a deep funk.

I woke the next morning, sore but satisfied. I was sprawled on my stomach with Rio's arm draped across my back. Rio slept on soundly, so I took my time in studying his features, committing his face to memory for when he wasn't here. The long, black eyelashes. Slightly parted lips. His messy, dirt-blond hair. I didn't want to forget a single detail: especially not those sea-blue eyes, which were suddenly wide open and looking right at me.

"I could feel you watching me," he said with a sleepy smile. "You're such a perv."

"Hey, a man needs something in the wank-bank for when you're on the other side of the world." I grinned at him, unashamed.

"What the hell for?" he retorted, rolling away from me. "Won't you be too busy fucking anything with a pulse?"

"Is that what you were mad about last night?" And there was me thinking he was annoyed because I said I was in love with him, when all along, the real reason was I'd told Riley I wouldn't hesitate to move on after Rio left. It was a lie, of course, but Rio didn't seem to realise that any more than Riley did. Was he really sulking because he didn't want me to fuck anyone else? Seriously, the ego of his man knew no bounds. "Don't tell me you won't be doing the same thing in America."

"Talking of America..." Rio said, pushing back the duvet and getting out of bed. "...I've got a band meeting this morning, so you need to get your lazy arse up and get dressed."

"You want me to come with you?"

It would be a surprise if he did. As far as I knew, he hadn't spoken to any of his bandmates and explicitly told them we were back together, even temporarily.

"Fuck, no!" he answered, a little more vehemently than was called for. "You're not exactly their favourite person."

"I'm not anybody's favourite person."

Which was true. I wasn't even Rio's, and he was the one fucking me.

"You're Dane's. That's why you should go and see him and put things right between you."

"Yeah, right. Not sure he's ready to listen."

"Then make him. Sit him down and explain, calmly and clearly, what this life is doing to you. He'll understand." Rio was adamant, and more than likely right. I just didn't want to face Dane if he was still angry with me. "I'll call you an Uber," Rio continued.

"I haven't said I'm going yet," I objected weakly.

I mean, I knew it needed to be done sooner rather than later, but the thought of discussing my problems with Dane was enough to make want a stiff drink or three. I was afraid once I started, I wouldn't be able to stop. Dane would never take me seriously if I showed up drunk, and Rio would give up on me altogether.

"You're going," Rio stated firmly, in a tone which implied there was no point arguing. "You need to sort this out."

"What about you?" I demanded petulantly. "Are you going to tell Cage and the others about me?"

Rio shrugged. "There's nothing to tell."

*Bastard.* He walked out of the bedroom, leaving me to scowl after in, angry and confused. Had I made a mistake coming here? Moving into his house, even in the short term? All Rio did, was contradict himself and bamboozle me. He didn't want me, but he didn't want anyone else to have me. He didn't love me, but he didn't like it when I said as much to other people. He wanted Dane and Riley to know we were together but wasn't prepared to tell his own friends. How was I supposed to know where I stood with the man from one minute to the next?

Then again, my being here wasn't permanent, was it? A couple of weeks and Rio would be gone again. Out of my life and shagging his way across North America. What difference did it make, what he did and said now? The end result was always going to the same. Rio would leave and I would be alone again.

I took my time getting dressed and using the bathroom. Partly to delay the inevitable face to face with Dane, and partly to frustrate Rio, who would be growing more impatient by the minute as he waited for me to appear. If he wanted to play games, it was fine by me. He wasn't going to get all his own way, though.

Shit. We really didn't belong together, did we? Not when we couldn't go two minutes without pissing each other off or saying crap that was designed to deliberately hurt the other's feelings. It would be better for both of us if I just moved out now, but I couldn't bring myself to do it. Whatever he thought of me, I loved Rio and I wanted – no, *needed* – to spend this time with him, however painful it turned out to be in the long run.

"Your Uber is here," Rio said, as soon as I showed my face in the kitchen.

"Don't I get time for a coffee?"

"Up to you. You're paying." He smirked. "I only said I'd order it for you."

"Yeah, to go somewhere I don't want to go," I complained, annoyed at being out-smarted again. No matter what I did, Rio was always one step ahead of me. "Fine. Whatever. Have a nice time *not* telling your mates about me."

I grabbed my phone and stormed out. It was a relatively short distance to Dane's house, but the journey was made longer by the sheer volume of traffic on the roads. It gave me a chance to calm down if nothing else. If I barged into Dane's still angry, it would lead to another fight, and nothing would be resolved. How was I supposed to resolve anything, anyway, when I had no clue what I was doing with my life? For once though, I needed to be strong and not let someone else dictate what I should do.

Dane answered the door, dressed in a t-shirt and fleece lined jogging bottoms. He didn't smile. He simply turned and walked back along the hallway, not questioning that I would follow like the faithful little puppy dog he obviously believed me to be.

"Is that Dozer's car outside?" I asked, curious as to why our drummer would be at Dane's house at that time of day.

"Yes," Dane answered shortly without turning round.

He turned into the study, and I stopped dead in the doorway, Dozer wasn't the only one of my bandmates in the room. KP and Nelson were there too, as well as Jaded Intent's official manager. I used the term 'official', because everyone knew Dane was the real power behind the throne. He was the one calling the shots and pulling the strings. Mike Campbell was little more than a figurehead.

"If this is an intervention, you're a bit late," I remarked dryly. "You're supposed to act *before* I try to kill myself. Not after."

"You mean you did jump into the river deliberately," Dane said. "Why did you tell Rio it was an accident?"

"Because it was!" I fired back in irritation. "That's not what I was on about. I've been drinking myself into an early grave for months. Where were you lot then?"

"We're here now," Mike spoke up, apparently finding a voice – and a backbone – of his own for once. "I've got you into a brilliant rehab centre, so don't worry... we'll soon have you back to normal."

"I'm not going to fucking rehab," I retorted, laughing in their faces. "I don't need it."

"What do you need then?" Dane ground out furiously. "And don't say Rio, because he's the cause of all this in the first place. He's no fucking good for you, Garrison, and you know it."

"Of course, I know it! Just like I know I'm going to get hurt all over again when he leaves, but guess what? Knowing doesn't stop me loving him." I ran my hands through my short hair in exasperation. "But this isn't about Rio. Don't you get it? It's about me."

"Everything is always about you, Garrison," Nelson said flatly. "To be honest, we're sick of it."

"Nelson!"

"No, Dane. He needs to be told and it needs to be now, because who knows how long it will be before he's sober enough to listen to us again."

I sank into an empty chair and leaned forward, elbows on knees, face in hands. Things were worse than I thought if the other guys were ready to turn against me. But if they really were tired of putting up with me and my drunken shenanigans, why bother putting up a fight to keep me in the band? They ought to be glad they were getting rid of me at long last. Still, I couldn't deny it stung a little to hear they were sick of me.

Lifting my head, I sought out Dane's concerned gaze. At the end of the day, his was the only opinion that mattered. His blessing was the only one I needed for me to be able to leave Jaded Intent with a clear conscience.

"Please," I said wearily, "can you just try and understand? I can't do this anymore. I don't want any of it. I don't want to be the fucked-up person that I am now. I don't want suicide to be the only way of escaping this life. I'm miserable, Dane. I've been miserable for a long time, since way before Rio came along. He made it worse, yes, but I was already a mess, and you know it."

There was silence in the room, and I looked each of them in the eye in turn, pleading with them to see sense. One way or another, Jaded Intent were going to lose me. It was up to them if they lost me to a seaside cottage or a coffin. I'd stay if they insisted, but it was only a matter of time before I opted to end it once and for all. I didn't say it out loud, because it would feel too much like emotional blackmail, but if I loved them enough to stay, couldn't they find it within themselves to love me enough to let me go?

"Maybe I sound like an ungrateful brat," I continued, when they all sat there staring at me without saying anything, "because I know there are thousands of guys out there who would kill for the chance at the life I have, but I'm done, guys. I want to sit by the sea and write songs. I want the inside of my head to be peaceful, instead of the never-ending cacophony I hear now. And, with or without you guys – with or without Rio – I just want to be happy. Is that really too much to ask?"

More silence. The guys looked at each other. Looked at Dane. Looked back at me.

"Can somebody say something?"

"You'll still do the album?" Dane asked finally.

"Yeas, I told you I would. I'm not just going to ditch you guys."

"And we get first dibs on anything you write?"

"I don't know how to write for anyone else."

Dane crossed the room and grabbed my wrist, pulling me to my feet and into an enormous bear hug. L leaned against him, resting my head on his shoulder. The others – with the exception of Mike – hurried over to join us, making us into one giant heap of Jaded Intent. We stood that way for the longest time. Long enough for me to start to feel smothered. Even so, I had no intention of pulling away and being the first one to break this demonstrable bond of unity.

"Guess we're looking for a guitarist then," Dane said gruffly, his voice cracking with emotion. "But if you change your mind and want to come back, you just say the word."

"Wait a minute," Mike interrupted, "I'm the manager of this band and I –"

"I think you'll find it's *my* band." Dane cut him off abruptly. "Mine and Garrison's. We founded this band, so if he wants to leave, he can. And if he wants to come back at any point, he can. Clear?" He turned back to face me. "I'm not happy about it, Garrison, but if it comes down to a choice of visiting you at some damn seaside cottage or laying flowers on your gravestone, there can only be one answer. I don't want to lose you, bro."

Impulsively, I threw myself into his arms and hugged him again. I was sad too. It was the end of an era, and of life as I knew it. But for the first time in ages, my heart felt lighter. I had hope and a bright future ahead of me. One where escaping my self-destructive lifestyle didn't involve suicide.

# Chapter Thirteen

THE TIME PASSED way too fast for my liking. I was counting down the days until Rio left, trying to pretend it didn't bother me as much as it really did. If Rio cared at all, he was better than me at not showing it. It would be hard to describe what we had as a loving relationship. Most of the time, we barely managed to be civil to each other. And sex was never about making sweet, sweet love. It was hot and heavy, angry hate-sex. I didn't mind too much, not even when it left me sore and aching afterwards.

A bit of discomfort was a price worth paying when it meant I got what came next. Lying in bed, sated and spent, was the only time Rio let his guard down. Dane would piss himself laughing if he knew, but those lazy moments spent cuddling with Rio were the best. Those were the moments I lived for. Finding his arm draped across my stomach and one leg wedged between mine, was the best reason I could think of for waking up in the morning.

The trouble was, I knew I was heading for another unhealthy dose of depression when he wasn't around to hold me anymore. I just hadn't decided what to do about it. Going down the route of therapy and medication didn't really appeal, and Dane was bound to drive me crazy with his over-the-top mothering act. I guess, at some point, I was going to have man up and get the fuck over Rio Darke.

During the day, I spent a lot of time with Dane and the other guys, thrashing out the songs for Jaded Intent's new album. Currently, we had a list of twenty-seven songs that needed to be whittled down to sixteen. Most of the songs came from Dane and KP. A few were mine, but I hadn't really been in the right frame of mind for writing over the past few months, so what I had managed to produce wasn't all that good anyway. The guys were trying to find a way of dropping my songs from the list without upsetting me. I hated the way they felt as though they had to walk on eggshells around me, like one wrong word would have me reaching for a blade and slitting my wrists. They needn't have worried. I was aware my songs were a load of shit, even if my pride wouldn't allow me to admit it to the others. The best I could do, was quietly support the alternative options and not make a big deal out of the fact that – for the first time ever – a Jaded Intent album would not feature a single track written by yours truly.

A couple of times, I hung out at the rehearsal studio with Rio and the guys from Carnival. They made it clear from the start that I was not entirely welcome. Cage – who I had been friendly with once upon a time – wouldn't even look at me, let alone speak to me. Juno and Carter acted like I was a bad smell under their noses, while Mal kept giving me the side-eye, like he was plotting against me somehow.

Other days, when Dane and Riley were off doing their own thing, and Rio was quite blatant in his unwillingness to take me with him, I slowly and reluctantly packed up the stuff I had at Rio's. I hired a removals company to pack up my apartment and put everything into storage, seeing as I had no intention of ever returning there. Once it was empty, I would put it on the market and start looking for my dream cottage by the sea. Life was changing rapidly, and I had to keep reminding myself it was a good thing. It was what I wanted. My choice.

All except for Rio leaving, of course.

The penultimate morning of our time together was bittersweet. I woke, the little spoon to Rio's big spoon. His arm was tight around my chest, the palm of his hand over my heart. A heart that was already heavy with missing him, even though he was yet to leave. He was still mine for another twenty-four hours, although I was both sad and annoyed that he wouldn't be spending every second of the fleeting time with me.

I didn't move, taking what I could get for as long as I could. These few precious moments, when we were both pretending I was still asleep were everything. They were the moments when Rio was not afraid to show me affection. For a few blissful seconds, I could believe he loved me for me, and not just as a convenient body to keep his bed warm.

His lips grazed my shoulder. A final squeeze. A sigh, and then...

"I know you're awake."

"If I lie, and tell you I'm still asleep, can we stay like this? Just for another five minutes?"

What I really meant was *just forever,* but this situation was hard enough. I didn't need to embarrass myself by begging. *Don't leave me. Stay. Love me. Let me love you. Love me. Love me. Please just love me.* I didn't say any of what I was thinking, of course, all too aware that any outpouring of desperation would send him running for the hills.

"Except you've already proved you're awake by answering," Rio said, although he remained pressed against my back, his arm wound tightly around me.

I fake snored and he laughed softly.

"Anyone ever tell you impossible?"

"Only my whole life," I replied, smiling because it was true. "Although, mainly by you these days."

"Well, that's because you are." His huff of amusement was warm against the back of my neck.

And still, he hadn't pulled away. Was it because he didn't want this to end either? Or was I reading too much into it? Kidding myself he had feelings for me that simply weren't there?

I twisted around to face him, pushing my luck, but Rio gave me a lazy smile and stayed put. Not panicking and backing away when he felt threatened by any degree of intimacy that wasn't straight up fucking.

"Make love to me," I said, hating the doubt and uncertainty in my voice. Hating even more, that I could see the same emotions reflected in the brilliant blue of his eyes. But there I was, pleading with him, despite promising myself I wasn't going to.

"You're insatiable." He shook his head and rolled his eyes, but it wasn't exactly a no, was it? Not when he was lying there, so close I could kiss him with the slightest tilt of my head. "Aren't you sore from last night?"

"I'm fine," I lied. I'd probably be feeling the effects of last night for days. Rio was never what you might call gentle. But I didn't want anyone else after him. I had to take as much as he would give me and make it last. "I'm a big boy. I can take it."

"I'm bigger." Rio smirked.

He closed the gap between our mouths and kissed me, unexpectedly sweet and caring for Rio. I brought my hand up to his face and cupped his cheek. His hand trailed slowly down my body, his fingers dipping between my buttocks. I moaned into his mouth as the deepened, then yelped in pain as he stabbed a finger into my tender hole.

"Ow! What the fuck, Rio?"

He smirked again, totally unconcerned at having deliberately caused me discomfort.

"If you can't take a finger," he said smugly, "there's no way you can take my monster dick."

"Monster dick? Seriously?" I scowled and punched him in the shoulder.

"It's bigger than yours."

"Yeah, well, that's not saying much, because mine is tiny," I scoffed. "Like really, really tiny. What? Wait... what the fuck am I saying?"

"You're such an idiot!" Rio practically creased up with laughter. "I'm going to call you Needledick from now on."

I grinned back at him, realising how much I had missed this. Lying in bed. Teasing. Laughing. Enjoying each other's company. It was the way we used to be, before I ruined everything by blowing some random guy I didn't even remember. *This* was what I wanted back. I mean, hot and heavy sex was great and all that, but being with him – like we the only two people in the world – that's what made my heart sing.

I gasped in pleasant surprise as Rio's fingers curled around my dick, which – naturally – rocketed from semi to rock hard at warp speed.

"Hmm, doesn't feel that small to me," he mused, a thoughtful expression on his face as he fondled me. "But the proof, as they say, is in the tasting."

He waggled his eyebrows suggestively. I didn't think that was the saying or what it meant, but who was I to argue? What was I going to tell him? That he couldn't suck me off until he got his proverbs correct? Hell to the no on that score!

"Sixty-nine?" Rio asked.

Which would be a hell to the *yes*!

All it took was a nod and Rio whisked the duvet from the bed and rearranged himself with such indecent haste that I couldn't help laughing.

"Hey, you'd better not be laughing at the mighty love-sausage," Rio said indignantly, trying his hardest to keep a straight face and making me laugh even harder. He bucked his hips, giggling like a schoolboy as he waved his dick in my face. "You've hurt his feelings. I think you should kiss him better."

"I can do better than that," I retorted, swallowing him to the root.

For the next few minutes, the room was filled with the sound of slurping, sucking and muffled moans as we gorged ourselves on each other. Embarrassingly, I was the first to shoot my load. I tried to warn Rio, but he sealed his lips around my dick and sucked me dry.

"What about you?" I asked in a daze, when he released me with a wet pop. "You didn't come."

"I'm about to."

He rolled me onto my back and straddled my thighs, vigorously pumping his dick until he spurted warm ropes of spunk over my chest and stomach. Then he bent low over my body, licking my way up my torso and ending in a searing kiss. He pushed his come into my mouth with his tongue.

"Fair's fair," he murmured softly, pressing our foreheads together.

"Also incredibly gross, but hot as fuck," I told him with a broad smile.

But, oh God, why did we have to wait until it was too late for us to realise we could be happy together? We could have been content in our relationship weeks ago, instead of pissing it up the wall in fits of jealousy and resentment and being too bloody stubborn to admit we were in love. Well, I'd admitted to it countless times. Rio was the one who refused to tear down the barricade he'd built around his heart. I was happy, but sad at the same time, because I felt as though I was losing him again, when I'd only just found the real Rio.

"I need to shower," he said, peeling himself off my sticky chest. "And you need to call a taxi."

"Why?" I stretched my arms above my head and gave him a puzzled look. "Where are we going?"

"*We're* not going anywhere," he replied, avoiding my gaze. "You're going to Dane's."

"Not until tomorrow."

"It will be better if you go today. I'll have a lot to do in the morning and it will be easier without you moping around and getting in the way."

"You're kicking me out?" I leapt from the bed in a blind rage and began pulling on yesterday's clothes. It was a struggle, because I didn't seem able to coordinate my arms and legs, which only served to increase my agitation. "You're fucking unbelievable!"

"So are you!" Rio retorted, running his hands through his hair in frustration. "Jesus Christ, Garrison, why does every conversation with you have to end in a fight?"

"Oh, I don't know, Rio." my eyes were hot and stinging and I ground the heels of my hands into them, determined not to cry in front of him. "Maybe it's because we just had amazing sex and now you're dumping me before your dick is even dry."

Rio rolled his eyes. "I'm not dumping you, for fuck's sake."

"No, because we'd have to be together first. Why did you bring me here, when you never wanted me in your home?" I cast a desperate look around the room for my boots, but it was hard to see anything clearly through the film of tears that blurred my vision. *Don't cry. Don't fucking cry.* "And you're the one who starts a fight every time I say I love you."

"You're here because I was trying to help you after that dumb suicide shit you pulled," Rio cried in exasperation. "And, for your information, I don't get mad every time you say you love me. I get mad when you say I don't love *you*!"

"Well, that's just... hold on..." I stared at him, suddenly confused. "What do you mean?"

"Every fucking time," Rio continued, still standing there – gloriously butt-naked. "It doesn't matter whether you're talking to me, Dane, Riley or anyone else. You tell them I don't love you. That I don't want you. You're so fucking wrong."

He walked over to the end of the bed and sat down, elbows on knees and face in hands. I stared at him, nonplussed, my anger deflating instantly.

"Are you telling me that you *are* in love with me?"

He nodded miserably and I regarded him with uncertainty. Could I believe him? Because why make his grand revelation now, when he would be leaving in twenty-four hours? And why order me to go, instead of wanting to spend one more night with me? I didn't know what to say, so I reverted to type and blurted out the wrong thing.

"You've got a funny way of showing it."

"I thought I just did." He gestured to the rumpled sheets behind him. "You know what we did was different. Not the sucking each other off, but the stuff before it... that was love, Garrison."

Lost and bewildered, I sank to the floor, close to him, but not touching. Suddenly, I felt so tired and sad. I didn't understand this thing between us, and I probably never would.

"Why do we keep doing this to each other?"

"I don't know." He dropped his hands from his face, but kept his gaze firmly fixed on the carpet at his feet. "Maybe Dane was right all along. You and me – we don't work."

"But we could," I said plaintively. "Why not if we love each other?"

"Because sometimes..." Rio answered, raising his head so that his eyes met mine. "... love isn't enough."

# Chapter Fourteen

LATER THAT SAME MORNING, Dane walked into his luxurious living room, humming softly to himself. Everything in the room was white. Carpet, walls, furniture, all white, with only one small piece of minimalist art over the fireplace, where anyone else would have a mega-size flat-screen TV. I strongly suspected the décor was more to Riley's taste than Dane's. The Dane I knew couldn't care less about the colour of paint on the walls, but he doted on Riley, and what the younger man wanted, he got in bucket loads.

Dane took a phone charger from a drawer and strolled back across the room. He reached the door and paused. He turned slowly, finally noticing me curled up on his sofa.

"Uh... hi?" he said, bemused. "I wasn't expecting to see you until tomorrow."

"Change of plan."

"Okay." He regarded me solemnly for a moment. "You want to talk about it?"

I nodded pathetically, my eyes flooding with the tears I'd fought so hard to hold back since leaving Rio's house.

"Fuck," Dane muttered. "Something tells me I'm going to need a stiff drink for this shit and it's not even lunchtime." His cheeks reddened as he realised what he'd said. "Stiff coffee. Strong coffee. That's what I meant. Stay here. I'll be right back."

Resting my head back on the cushion, I closed my eyes and sighed. They meant well, but Dane and the others were never going to stop treating me like I was made of fucking glass. Like I'd shatter if they looked at me funny. It was nice they cared, but I was sick of it. And I knew they were all waiting for me to fall to pieces without Rio.

"Garrison?"

My eyes snapped open. Dane stood over me, his handsome face etched with concern, and a steaming mug of coffee in each hand. He held one out to me and I took it gratefully.

"Go on then." Dane plonked his backside down beside me, even though the sofa was easily eight feet long and could accommodate the whole band twice over. "What did he do this time?"

"He told me that he loves me," I said miserably.

Dane shook his head in mock disapproval. "The bastard."

"You don't understand," I complained bitterly. "You never did."

"I understand you and Rio spend half your lives fucking and the other half trying to rip each other to shreds. that's not my idea of love, nor anybody else's.

"Maybe it's ours, though. Mine and Rio's. We want to love each. We just don't know how."

"So, you keep on hurting each other instead?" Dane's eyebrows knitted together in a deep frown. "it's not healthy, Garrison. Surely you can see how toxic your so-called relationship is?"

"Don't talk to me like a child," I said irritably. "I don't pass comment on you and Riley, do I? At least Rio is the same age as me. Besides, it's not always toxic between us. We have our moments."

Dane narrowed his eyes, pissed off by my jab at the age gap between him and Riley. But if he wanted to chat shit about my relationship, I would sure as hell give it right back.

"Actually, you've made a lot of derogatory remarks about Riley. Mostly when you're drunk, but they still count." He leaned back with a smirk. "And, if by moments you mean all the hate sex you guys have – *that* doesn't count for shit."

"How do you...?"

"Rio told me, dumbass. The only way he can get it up for you is if he's angry, which should really tell you something."

I blinked back a fresh wave of tears and looked away from him. It wasn't the first time he'd seen me cry over Rio, so I didn't care about that. I just hated the thought Dane was right. I wasn't ready to accept the fact I'd been nothing more than a convenient shag all along.

"I'm sorry," Dane said, nudging my arm. "I'm supposed to be supporting you, not making you feel worse."

"It's not your fault," I replied, leaning forward to put mu untouched coffee on the low table. Sitting back again, I hugged my knees to my chest. "You don't know him like I do. He's different when it's just us. Knock-down fights and hate sex aside, he cares for me. I know he does."

"I know you *want* him to care," Dane said with a sigh, "and I'm not saying this to be cruel, but I don't see it happening. Ever."

"It already happened," I argued. "Today... this morning... we were the closest we've ever been. He told me he loved me, but then..."

"See, this is what I mean." Dane sounded exasperated. "If he loved you, there wouldn't be a *but then*. Rio should want to spend every last minute of today with you. Wait..." Dane gave me a suspicious look. "You didn't run away because he used the L-word, did you?"

"No, of course I didn't. I mean, I ran, yeah, but that wasn't the reason."

"Why then?"

"Because as soon as he got through telling me how much he loves me, he told me to leave. He said you were right about us, and that we would never work." Unable to sit still any longer, I leapt to my feet and began to pace up and down in front of the coffee table. Holy fuck, did I need a drink and I wasn't talking about coffee. The only thing keeping me from reaching for a bottle was the dream of my little seaside cottage. Without that I had nothing. I couldn't afford to let the booze suck me back under.

"Look, I get that you're hurting right now," Dane said, watching me closely, as though he was worried I was about to make a dash for the nearest knife drawer, "but I need to know if... you know... feel the urge to..."

"The urge to what?" I stopped pacing and turned to glare at him. "Fart? Sneeze? What?"

"You don't need to be such an arsehole about it."

"Nor do you," I snapped. "I'm not suicidal, Dane. I'm just sad. I can be sad without wanting to kill myself, can't I?"

Dane got to his feet and walked around the coffee table to stand in front of me. He liked to be face to face while he did his best friends and brothers for life, happy-clappy bullshit.

"I'm worried about you, okay. If you can be sad, I can worry."

Which would mean more if he didn't worry about every person on the whole fucking planet. Look what he'd done for his cousin a few months back, getting CJ and his band a recording contract, and paying for CJ's boyfriend to go to rehab. Christ, Dane even bought Boone a guitar, having never met him. Dane cared about everyone, so I was nothing special, other than for the fact I probably pissed him off more than anyone else.

"To tell you the truth," Dane continued, "and please don't take this the wrong way... I'm glad he saw sense and changed his mind about taking you to the party tonight. You know what Carnival parties are like. They descend into chaos every single time. Drink, drugs and fighting are not what you need to be around right now. That's why CJ is keeping Boone away."

I stared at him blankly before I remembered his cousin's band were going on tour with Carnival as the support act. Obviously, it was not the only thing to have slipped my mind, because I'd forgotten all about Carnival's tradition of throwing a wild, hedonistic party the night before they set off on tour. I'd been to a few of them over the years, and usually ended up getting trashed with Cage, whose penchant for drugs and alcohol equalled my own. This one, though, I knew nothing about. Mainly because Carnival's guitarist – the man I'd been living with for the past few weeks – neglected to tell me it was happening.

"Where are they having this party?" I asked stiffly.

Dane took a step back and folded his heavily corded arms across his massive chest. He frowned again, as it sank in that he had inadvertently let something slip that he shouldn't have. He'd probably claim it was Rio's fault for not telling me. Or, at least, for not telling Dane that he hadn't told me. Something along those lines, anyway. Such trains of thought tended to make my head ache.

"It doesn't matter where it is," Dane stated firmly, "because you're not going."

"You don't get to tell me I can't go," I retorted. "You're not my dad."

"Thank fuck for that," came his emphatic and swift response.

I didn't blame him. I wouldn't want to be my father either. Not because it meant having me for a son, but because my old man was a prick. The dislike was mutual, which was why it was years since I last saw him and had no intention of rectifying that fact any time soon. It would suit me just fine if I never laid eyes on the guy again. Mum was okay, I guess. I made the effort to visit her at least once a year, but she lived with my brother and his family these days, and Corben was the same level of douchebag as our sorry excuse for a father. I was closer to Dane's family than my own, even when Dane decided to go all mother-hen on me, like he was now.

"Rio didn't mention it, did he?" Dane asked tiredly. "He doesn't want you there. I'm sorry, but it's the truth. I'm trying to give him the benefit of the doubt and believe he's doing it for your sake."

"What? You think he doesn't want me there cramping his style?"

Because that was exactly what I was thinking. How stupid did I have to be to buy into Rio's I-love-you-really bullshit? He'd said what he thought I wanted to hear, so I would leave without causing him any trouble. To keep me from kicking off when I found out he was fucking someone else, unable to wait a whole twenty-four hours, apparently, when he was in another country, and I wouldn't know who was in his bed.

"Don't put words in my mouth," Dane said, but there was scepticism in his tone and in his eyes. "But you know what Rio is like."

"I'm going to that party," I ground out, determined.

"The fuck you are!" Dane fired back. "I'll lock you in your room if that's what I have to do to keep you here."

"The door doesn't even have a lock, you dick."

The way he was glaring at me, I wouldn't put it past him to go and buy one. Either that, or hire some big, meathead security goon to stand in the corner of the room and prevent me leaving. Mind you, if I capitulated too easily, Dane wouldn't buy it and he'd watch me like a hawk anyway. He had to believe I was going to fight him every step of the way. Cue one typical Garrison-style tantrum.

I stomped my feet and raged. Called him every name under the sun, including a choice few I didn't often stoop to using. By the time I told him I was going to my room, and he could go fuck himself, Dane was relieved to see me go.

Secluded in what was now my permanent residence – at least until I bought cottage by the sea and moved out for good – I pulled out my phone and scrolled through the short list of contacts. Who to call? That was the dilemma. It wasn't like I had a long list to choose from, thanks to my previous indiscretions with other people's numbers. The few names I did have either wouldn't know where the party was being held, or they wouldn't tell me. A lot of our mutual friends and acquaintances were all too aware of mine and Rio's strained relationship. They knew I'd been staying with him these past weeks. It was only natural they would question why Rio wasn't taking me to Carnival's farewell bash as his guest, and then they would come to the same conclusion as Dane. Rio didn't want me there.

And the simple fact was, most of those friends and acquaintances liked Rio a lot more than they liked me. Nobody would tell me shit if it meant pissing off Rio.

I guess I could call Rio himself, but we'd already said our goodbyes. If he really didn't want me at the party – whether it was for my sake or his – he wouldn't be happy if I started begging for an invite. Not that he would be any happier if I turned up without one.

I had to know, though. Was he doing it to protect me? To keep me safe from the evils of drugs and alcohol? Or was I already a distant memory, our time together nothing more than a sexually gratifying way of passing the time? I needed to know if I meant anything to him. If I didn't... then what was the point in anything anymore?

# Chapter Fifteen

BEING famous did have some perks. Like calling up places where Carnival had hosted previous parties and pretending I wanted to book a room for after that night's event. Once I dropped my name into the conversation, whoever I was speaking to was all too keen to help, even if it was only to say I had the wrong venue and there was no party. A couple of the less eager to oblige establishments informed me in no uncertain terms that the members of Carnival and their guests were permanently banned from the premises after the last party they'd held all but destroyed the property.

Eventually, I connected with some sweet, naïve, young thing who could barely contain her excitement over all the famous rock-stars she would be meeting later. It turned out she was a huge Jaded Intent fan too, so talking to the one and only Garrison was the icing on the cake as far as she was concerned. The poor girl was practically beside herself with guilt when she told me the hotel was fully booked.

"It doesn't matter," I said truthfully. I never wanted a room anyway, only affirmation the hotel was where I would find Rio partying the night away without me.

*So long as he wasn't partying with anyone else, everything would work out just fine.*

"What's your name?" I asked her. "How would you like it if I brought you some signed merchandise later?"

"Really? Oh, my God, that would be fantastic!" she squealed in excitement. My name's Layla. Can you sigh it *with love*? My friends will be so jealous."

If I remembered rightly, Dane had several boxes of Jaded Intent merchandise stored in his garage. Whatever I picked out, it would have to be worth something, because the lovely Layla wasn't likely to keep her job much longer if she didn't stop fangirling over the high-profile guests. I should try and set her up with stuff she could sell for a few quid on eBay.

I knelt on the floor beside the boxes and began to sort through them. Hell, I didn't know if the assortment of t-shirts, hoodies, caps, posters, mugs and crap had any real value. We charged a small fortune for it at our concerts and online, but it looked like a load of old tat to me. Although, I did come across a Jaded Intent mug which made me smile, because it reminded me of the one in Rio's bathroom at the cottage. At first, I thought he'd kept it as a memento of our previous relationship, but – and it was a minor detail – perhaps it was proof that he had loved me at one time.

"What are you doing?"

I added the mug to the growing pile of items I'd selected for Layla and glanced up at Dane. My best friend had suspicion written all over his face and my insides tightened uncomfortably. What had I done to lose his trust after being like brothers for so many years? And when I had lost it? Obviously, I'd been drunk to see it happening right in front of my eyes.

The real question – the one I ought to be asking – was could I win back his trust or was it gone for good? It was probably going to require a lot of hard work on my part, if I was going to prove myself to him, and I was prepared to do whatever was necessary. But not today. Today, I was about to lie to him. Big time. It was hardly an auspicious start on the road to redemption.

"I'm grabbing a few bits to take to a fan. She's... sick. In hospital."

"So, why are you doing it?" Dane narrowed his eyes in doubt, trying to suss out what game I was playing this time. I guess it was no surprise he didn't believe me. "How come I haven't heard about her?"

"Because this isn't about you," I answered evenly. "The rest of us have fans too, you know."

"Fair enough, but since when did you care about the fans? Unless you're shagging them, of course." His eyes narrowed even further. "Please tell me you haven't impregnated some poor, misguided, young woman."

"Not likely," I retorted. "That's your department. What's happening with your latest paternity suit anyway?"

"Uh, there has only been one, thank you very much. There's no *latest* about it. And nothing happened, because she was proved to be lying and the case was dropped."

"You should sue the bitch for every penny," I said.

"What would that achieve?" Dane shook his head. "I don't need the money and she obviously does. The woman is already in a desperate situation. I'm not about to make her life worse."

I snorted. "You're too nice."

"And you're trying to change the subject," he said, crouching down in front of me. "Don't think I didn't notice. What are you up to, Garrison?"

"I told you. I'm signing all this shit and taking it to a fan."

"Has she got a name, this mysterious fan of yours?"

"Well, obviously she has a name. Layla." I held up a glossy black and white photo of the two of us. "Hey, you should sign this as well. We all know your signature is worth more than mine."

"Aren't you the one who just said this isn't about me?"

I stuck my tongue out at him and he laughed. That was the thing with Dane. He could never stay mad at me for long. I hated lying to him, especially when I was sober and had no excuse. If he knew what I was really planning though, he would feel duty bound to try and stop me, and I couldn't let that happen. My heart and soul were crying out to see Rio one last time.

"You're such a child," he said condescendingly.

"I think you must be mistaking me for your boyfriend," I taunted. "How old is he again?"

We gathered up an armful of goodies and carried them into the house to find a marker pen. We sat in Dane's study for an impromptu autograph session, accompanied by some good-natured ribbing. Dane relaxed a bit as we worked our way through the pile of merchandise. He still didn't entirely believe me, but he would do anything for our fans, so he was happy to go along with my Cock and Bull story for now.

"Maybe I should come with you," he said casually, once we had finished applying our monikers to everything we possibly could.

"Alternatively, you could let me go alone," I responded dryly. "I'm doing what you wanted and trying to move on. I don't need you to hold my hand every step of the way."

"I'm not trying to," he argued. "I was just thinking of this girl, Layla. Imagine how happy she'll be if both of us turn up."

"Probably not very. I mean it. She likes me, not you. In fact, I'm pretty sure she mentioned something about not liking you at all."

Dane arched his eyebrows. "Okay, so why have me sign all this shit?"

"Because you and I both know this stuff is going straight on eBay and, like I said earlier, your John Hancock is worth more than mine."

"You're a cynical bastard at times."

"But you love me anyway."

"Yeah, I do. Can't seem to help myself." He sighed. "Are you really okay with this whole Rio business?"

"No, but I'm doing the best I can. Just let me deal with it in my own way."

I was lying to him. *Again.* Because I had no intention of getting over Rio, and my way of dealing with it was by stalking the guy to a party he'd made it clear he didn't want me to attend.

It was Rio's fault anyway. If he had bothered to take a single moment out of his oh-so-busy schedule to explain – to tell me there was a party, but he didn't think it was healthy for the new, sober me to be there – I would have understood. Appreciated the fact he was trying to protect me and cared enough about me to shield me from the sheer depravity a Carnival party entailed.

Of course, it was far more likely I would have sulked, cried and thrown a strop of epic proportions on the assumption he didn't want me at his stupid party so he could screw around behind my back.

All of that was my business, though, not Dane's. He would accept I was trying, because it was what he wanted to believe. He probably had his big sausage-fingers crossed I would be more inclined to see reason once I was away from Rio and would change my mind about leaving the band.

Now was not the time to disillusion him, however. Not if I wanted to get out of the house without Dane accompanying me as an over-bearing chaperone.

"Want me to call you an Uber?" Dane asked, innocently, which implied he didn't fully trust me just yet.

"It's fine," I said lightly. "I need to start doing these things for myself."

Which was true enough, but also, if Dane made the call, he'd want to know which hospital and I didn't know what to say. Even if I did, I didn't want to end up miles away from the hotel. I mean, it would be easy enough to get another Uber from whatever hospital I went to, but what if Dane checked up on me? Or he could involve our management team, who would view visiting a sick fan as a huge promotional opportunity. To be fair, I, more than anyone, could do with some positive press right about now, but it wouldn't stay positive for long, would it? Not when it came out that I'd been lying all along and there was no fan.

Well, strictly speaking, there was. Layla was a real person and a real Jaded Intent fan, but she was hardly at death's door. Nobody would have anything good to say about me plying her with signed merchandise, once they learned I was only doing it to *get* to Rio.

Leaving Dane to brood over my true intentions, I went upstairs to my room and got changed. I put on tight leather pants – the ones Riley liked to tell me I was too old for – and a silk, silver-grey shirt. I added my black ankle boots with the pointed toes and used gel to push my short brown hair into soft spikes.

How could Rio resist such smokin' hotness? Maybe I wasn't a walking wet dream like he was, but I was looking pretty damn gorgeous, even if I did say so myself.

Dane looked me over from head to toe when I reappeared in the doorway to his study.

"That's a lot of effort for a fan," he remarked dryly. "Especially one of the female persuasion."

I shrugged, trying not to look like I'd just been caught out. Trouble was, we'd been friends for close to twenty-five years and a lot of the time, Dane knew me better than I knew myself. It was no secret that I swung both ways in the bedroom, but with a preference for men. Dane was all too aware that I seldom put an effort into looking good for women. Then again, I'd already told him this was not about sex.

"I haven't quit the band yet," I replied. "She'll be expecting the full Garrison experience."

"Aren't you forgetting something?" Dane ran his hand over my short hair, and I batted it away in irritation. "I could always give CJ a call. See if Boone still has that black wig."

"Ha! You think you're so funny, don't you? For the record, R... *I* like my hair like this." Fuck, I almost said Rio. Way to prove I was ready to move on from the guy. If Dane noticed my slip of the tongue, though, he chose not to mention it. "I should probably get going."

Dane nodded; his expression grim. He didn't believe me and – let's face it – he was right not to. At least this way, when it all went tits up and he had to haul my sorry arse out of trouble again, he would be justified in his self-righteous condemnation. It was how we rolled. I was the screw-up. He was the saint who was forced to put up with me.

"How long is this going to take?" Dane asked, as I grabbed the stuff and made a beeline for the front door.

"Couple of hours, maybe."

Another lie, because it was barely past noon and – even if the guys showed up early – Carnival parties were notorious for starting around ten at night, sometimes later.

"Garrison," Dane said, before I could close the door behind me. "Don't make me come looking for you."

"I won't," I promised.

And what do you know? Yet another fucking lie.

# *Chapter Sixteen*

**THE HOTEL WAS CLASSY.** Way too classy to host a Carnival party. I was surprised the lads' reputation hadn't preceded them and they hadn't been banned before they even set a foot in the door. No doubt the management thought the star-studded bash would be good for business. Guess they would find out the hard way how wrong they were. They would be lucky to have a hotel left by the end of the night if this turned into the typical Carnival style carnage.

There were three young women behind the reception desk. I made a beeline for the short, plump blonde at the far end. The one whose face lit up when I walked in. I put the box of signed merch on the desk in front of her.

"Layla, I assume," I said, with a seductive smile. Not that she stood a chance with me, but I'd long since learnt that flirting got you almost anywhere with gullible boys and girls. It was the dream, wasn't it? The sexy, rock star walking in and sweeping them off their feet? "As promised." I indicated the box, although she'd have to be blind not to have seen it already. "Dane signed some shit too."

I leaned on the desk casually, trying to look as though I belonged there, while Layla pawed through the items in the box. She was oblivious to the resentful looks her two colleagues were shooting in her direction. Did I feel bad that she'd probably be out of a job by the end of the day? Sure, but not enough to make me change my mind about what I was doing. The lovely Layla was a grown-up. She made her own decisions. How was it my fault if she made the wrong ones?

"So, um... I don't suppose you could let me into Rio Darke's room, could you?" I said sweetly, hoping what was in the box was enough to buy her loyalty. I'd throw in a kiss if it sealed the deal. Not so long back, I'd have given her a lot more besides, but these days I was faithful to Rio.

"Oh, I don't know if I should." Layla cast a sideways look at the other receptionists, her resolve wavering. "Mr. Darke isn't here yet. He might not like it."

"It's fine," I cajoled, leaning over the desk to whisper conspiratorially. "Look, not a lot of people know this, but Rio is my boyfriend. I want to surprise him."

"He is?" This time the doubtful look was aimed in my direction. "Well, I guess I could..."

"Garrison fucking Swann. What the hell are you doing here?"

I closed my eyes and cursed, before plastering on a fake smile and turning to face Cage Ramirez, Carnival's lead singer. We'd been friendly once, he and I, but not anymore. Cage had never forgiven me for the shit that went down with Rio three years ago. He was a few years older than me, and about the same height and build. His long, dark brown hair was past his shoulders and hung in his whisky-coloured eyes. If anything, Cage was even harder living than the rest of us. He was a heavy drinker, casual drug user, and serial shagger, who was currently going through his second divorce. Yet he still thought he was somehow better than me.

"Cage, why are you...? Oh, wait... is *this* where Carnival are having their party tonight? I had no idea. I was just bringing a few things to a fan."

Cage rolled his eyes. "I don't believe you."

"I can't help what you believe," I answered with a smirk, "and just because you don't believe it, doesn't make it any less true."

He grabbed my arm and propelled me across the foyer, away from the reception desk and the three curious pairs of ears behind it. I guess I was lucky he didn't throw me right out onto the street.

"You live with fucking Rio. You really expect me to believe he didn't tell you anything about tonight?"

"Funnily enough, it must have slipped his mind."

"Yeah, why do you think that is?" Cage sneered. "It's over, Garrison. He doesn't want you here. Time to accept it and move on."

"Sorry, you'll have to forgive me for not taking advice from a man who won't use a supermarket bag-for-life because it feels too much like commitment."

"Ha! You're funny."

Call me crazy, but his tone would suggest he was really thinking the exact opposite of what he said.

"When does Rio get here?" I asked belligerently.

It was a deliberate attempt to wind him up. As a rule, Cage didn't like being told no. Some deep, rooted childhood trauma – which none of us had ever fully understood because he'd never explained it to us – drove Cage's desire for adoration as much as it fuelled his reluctance to commit to anything or anyone other than Carnival. People walked on eggshells around him for fear of sending him into one of his violent rages, but I liked to buck the trend and push him to his limit. Because let's face facts – I was as fucked in the head as he was.

"What? Did he forget to tell you that too?" Cage cocked an eyebrow, refusing to rise to the bait for once. "Wow, he really does hate you, doesn't he?"

"Fuck off, Cage!" I scowled, because this wasn't the way this was supposed to go. Cage wasn't supposed to get the better of me, and Rio was supposed to be surprised and delighted when he walked in and found me waiting for him. "You don't know shit about me and Rio. Worry about your own relationship and stay out of mine. Oh, wait... isn't Chloe divorcing you? How many failed marriages does that make now?"

"Two, arsehole. How many times have you failed to keep hold of Rio?"

I smirked. "I haven't lost him yet."

"But you're about to," Cage said, sneering. "He won't stay faithful while he's on tour, anymore that you'll keep it in your pants waiting for him."

He was wrong about that. About me. I would be totally loyal to Rio. I would do the studio album with Jaded Intent and then start the search for a small cottage somewhere private. Somewhere away from the limelight and constant public scrutiny. At the end of the tour, Rio would come back to me, and we would build a life together. Cage and Dane could shove their doubts and disapproval up their respective arses.

There was a stir in the hotel entrance, a sudden electric charge in the air. I didn't need to look to know who had walked in. Wherever, whenever – the atmosphere always changed drastically the moment Rio arrived. The girls behind the reception desk stood up a little straighter and the other guests in the foyer stopped what they were doing to simply stare, even though nobody had paid any attention to me and Cage. We were every bit as famous as Rio, but nowhere near as aesthetically stunning.

Rio was halfway to the reception desk when he caught sight of me next to Cage. He changed course and steamed over to us, his expression a blend of anger and caution. Unfortunately, he didn't seem to be as pleasantly surprised as I'd hoped he would be.

"Cage." His eyes settled on me. "Garrison."

"Dane didn't tell me, if that's what you're thinking," I blurted out. "I mean... he might have accidently let slip there was a party... which you didn't tell me about, by the way... but he never told me where it was. I found out for myself."

"How?" Cage demanded, like he didn't believe me. Like he assumed I didn't have the brains to play detective and figure shit out on my own.

"It wasn't that hard," I told him. "You guys are banned from most places, so it was just a process of elimination."

"Stay here," Rio said, with a roll of his big baby blues. "I'll get my room key and then you and I are going to have a discussion about you being here."

Cage cast me a look filled with nothing but contempt and hurried after Rio. He would try to dissuade him from taking me up to his room, because we all knew what happened when there Rio, me and a bed were in the same space. It went without saying, my persuasion techniques far outweighed whatever Cage had to offer.

Rio checked in and sauntered back over to me, his overnight bag slung over one shoulder: ever the picture of poise and calm. He grabbed my arm and steered me into the waiting lift car. I cast a look over my shoulder and waggled my fingers at Cage, who was scowling after us.

"Don't wind him up," Rio snapped, as the doors closed. "You piss him off, but I'm the one who has to spend the next eight months on the road with him."

"You'll survive." I stroked a hand down his muscled arm provocatively. "Aren't you pleased to see me?"

"No, Garrison, I'm not." He slapped my hand away in annoyance. "We said our goodbyes this morning. Dane promised he would keep you away."

"This has nothing to do with Dane."

"What? You expect me to believe he wasn't the one who told you about tonight?"

"He didn't. Not intentionally, anyway. Then he categorically told me I was not allowed to come. I used my initiative and found out where you were going to be all by myself," I said sulkily. "It was a case of having to, because you told me jack-shit."

"Because I don't want you anywhere near this. You know what Carnival parties are like. How every single one descends into an orgy of drugs and alcohol. You're not ready to be around all that yet."

We reached his suite on the top floor. Rio stomped through to the bedroom and dropped his bag onto the bed. I trailed after him, not bothering to stop and appreciate our surroundings. If you stayed in one fancy hotel room, you'd stayed in them all. I didn't need to look around to know there would be a huge flat-screen TV, plush sofas, shag-pile carpet, a massive bed and gold leaf on just about everything.

"I'll be fine if I'm with you."

"I'm not babysitting you all night, Garrison. I need to socialise. Talk to people."

"And you can do that. I'm not going to stop you. I'm a grown man, Rio, and I'm not going to fuck this up. I can go a few measly hours without a drink."

"You sure about that?"

"Positive. So..." I threw myself onto the bed and peered up at him from beneath lowered eyelashes. "Are you going to fuck me or what?"

"Now *that,* I definitely remember doing this morning." Rio laughed. He held out his hand and pulled me up from the mattress when I accepted it. "Okay, you can stay, but no alcohol and no drugs. And stay clear of Cage. Mal too. They're nothing but trouble."

I shrugged. "Aren't we all?"

Chapter Seventeen

THERE WERE QUITE a few familiar faces at the party. Not all of them were pleased to see me. In fact, hardly anybody was. Most of them, I'd well and truly burnt my bridges with in one way or another. A few of them had been victims of the infamous lost phone saga. Maybe I deserved the cold shoulder from these people who had mistakenly placed their trust in me, but then again… maybe they only had themselves to blame. My heavy drinking was legendary. They should have known better than to trust me in the first place.

I understood why CJ, Boone and the rest of the Original Sin guys chose not to be there, although I wished they were. At least they liked me after I saved the show that landed them their record deal, even if it was only a little bit. Boone was still in recovery though, and CJ would never do anything to jeopardise his boyfriend's health and happiness. Henry and Cooper were both a bit on the shy side, and way too timid for a Carnival party. It would be a minor miracle if the younger, inexperienced band survived the tour unscathed.

And it would be another one if I survived tonight. Jesus, parties were fucking boring when a guy was sober. I was stood in a corner like an idiot, sipping lemonade, while Rio cruised the room. At least watching Rio was a pleasant way to pass the time. He was easily the hottest guy in the room and looked amazing in jeans so tight they looked as though they had been spray-painted onto his legs, and a shimmering black shirt that was close to being see-through.

Eventually, he made his way to my side. His bright smile failed to reach his eyes, which continued to scan the room, probably seeking someone more interesting to talk to than me.

"How are you holding up?" he asked, his gaze tracking a younger man as he crossed the room.

I scowled into my flat lemonade. "Who's he?"

"Who? Him?" Rio's feigned innocence wouldn't fool a blind man. "Oh, you mean the guy in the blue shirt. That's our new roadie. Kevin or something." Rio rolled his eyes. "I mean, who calls their kid Kevin in this day and age?"

"He doesn't look like a kid to me," I complained sourly.

If I ever officially became Rio's boyfriend, I'd make it a condition that he didn't have anyone on tour who was younger or better looking than me. Not like that would be enough to stop him, but it might slow him down a bit. Make him think twice about what he was doing.

"He's younger than either of us," Rio said, laughing. Why would he take my jealousy seriously, when in his book we weren't a couple, so I had no right to be jealous in the first place. "Look, as far as I know, he's straight. It doesn't matter either way, because he's not my type. So, just relax and have a good time, will you? You're the one who insisted on being here."

I nodded, slightly numb. There was not much in his statement I could argue against.

"Actually, I need a word with him," Rio said casually. He knew I wasn't going to like it, which was why he was suddenly avoiding looking at me. "You don't have to worry, it's just that he's responsible for my drum kit. I want to be sure he knows what he's doing."

"Yeah, well, I doubt they'd have given him the job if he didn't."

"Come on, Garrison. Turn the green-eyed monster act down a notch, eh? You'd do the same if it was your guitars."

He was right in a way. If it was my guitars, I'd want to know about the guy responsible for transporting them safely. It didn't make me feel any better about Rio leaving me to go chasing after him though.

"It's fine," I told him flippantly. "I need a piss anyway."

I put my glass down on an empty table and stalked away, trying to act like I wasn't bothered and fooling nobody. I caught sight of Cage as I headed toward the restroom, saw the sneer on his face. I ducked my head and kept walking. They were all waiting for me to fail and let Rio down again and I hated it. If anything made me want to get good and drunk, it was Rio's bandmates' shitty attitudes.

"Garrisuuuuun!" Mal bellowed as soon as I entered the bathroom, as though the gap between us was six miles instead of six feet. He drew out the last syllable of my name until he ran out of breath.

I liked Mal least of the Carnival members. He swore blind he was straight, but he was always grabbing my arse or trying to squeeze my dick. I'd seen him do the same to Rio and Cage. Everyone laughed it off and treated Mal's behaviour like it was one big joke, so I had to bite my tongue and go along with it. I was on shaky ground with the other members of Carnival as it was. To a man, they disapproved of me moving in with Rio, even temporarily. In fact, they disapproved of our whole relationship and of me in general. Punching out the bass player was not going to do me any favours.

"Thought you might want something stronger than that stupid lime and fucking lemonade you've been nursing all night," Mal said, dangling a clear plastic baggie of white powder in my face.

"It's good stuff," Mal's companion chimed in eagerly. He was just a lad, barely more than twenty years old. Judging by the state of them, they had sampled the goods already that night.

"Yeah, thanks for the offer, but I don't touch that shit anymore."

I hadn't touched hard drugs in years. In the early days of Jaded Intent's success, my coke habit spiralled out of control. Not only had it cost me a fortune, but it almost cost me my life. Dane's intervention landed me my first stint in rehab. Admittedly, I'd exchanged hard drugs for alcohol, but I maintained my stance – as I had always done – that I was in control of my drinking. It was different with coke, which was why I hadn't touched it since getting clean.

"I was forgetting," Mal sneered. "Saint Rio has got you totally pussy-whipped these days." He angled his head and frowned, pretending he was deep in thought as he looked me up and down. "Can you call it pussy-whipped when there's no pussy in the equation? It should be dick-whipped instead, is that it, Garrison? Has Rio got you dick-whipped?"

"Dick-whipped." Mal's young friend laughed hysterically. "That's hilarious. Because you're both dudes, right, and Rio whips you with his dick."

"Yeah, Garrison and every other fag he meets." Mal smirked, like he knew something I didn't.

Was I missing something? I thought Rio had been faithful to me over the past couple of months, but what if I was kidding myself? What if he hadn't been rehearsing for the tour all those times he'd left the house alone? We never said we were exclusive, but I thought it was implied by the fact we were living together. Unless, of course, Rio didn't see us as living together as a couple. Maybe he viewed me as nothing more than a temporary house-guest and was only fucking me because I was a convenient hole.

Some of my doubt must have shown on my face, because Mal let out a harsh laugh.

"Come on, Garrison, you know how it is. You've been on the road enough times to know the way it is. What goes on tour, fucks on tour."

Yeah, I knew. Been there. Fucked that. When I was on tour, I had a different shag in every city we went to, and Rio had a reputation for doing the same. In terms of being a total man-whore, Rio equalled me on every level. And then some. He wasn't going to change just because I was sat at home waiting for him.

"Changed your mind about taking a little snort yet?" Mal taunted, jiggling the baggie in front of me again.

"Fuck off, Mal." I pushed past him, making it as far as the door before I hesitated. I was losing Rio all over again. There was nobody left to care what state I got myself into. "Have you got any pills?"

Because pills were different, right? A couple of pills never did anyone any harm. I'd get a nice little buzz going and forget all about Rio breaking my heart for the second time.

"I've got some Oxy," Mal's nameless buddy said. I mean, presumably he had a name. I just didn't care enough to find out what it was. He put his hand in his pocket and produced several foil tabs. "How many do you want?"

"Two for now. If I want more later, I'll come and find you."

"All two will do is cure your fucking headache," Mal jeered, snatching the pills from the other guy's hand. "If you want to feel something, you need to take at least four."

"Fine. Whatever."

I didn't want to get high so I could feel shit. It was the exact opposite. I wanted to numb those pesky feelings that threatened to overwhelm me. I craved oblivion from the pain of knowing whatever I'd had with Rio was over. He was moving on without me again. I didn't want to be conscious enough to think about it.

I washed the pills down with lukewarm tap water, disappointed when there wasn't an instant hit like the one that followed a good slug of alcohol.

Leaving Mal and his young friend snorting lines from the marble counter-top next to the sink, I went back to the party. In my heart of hearts, I wanted Mal to be wrong about Rio reverting to his old habits as soon as he was rid of me. I hoped when I showed up at Rio's side, he would smile and put his arm around me. Maybe even tell me he'd missed me and was about to send out a search party because I'd been away from him too long.

The alternative, was I would find him a corner, getting cosy with the cute new roadie. So much for the guy being straight. Rio had obviously lied to me, and he'd lined up my replacement already. Hadn't even waited until he was officially on tour. Rio threw back his head and laughed at something the guy said. The roadie placed his hand on the small of Rio's back, leaning in close to whisper into Rio's ear. There was no question in my mind. This guy would be in Rio's bed by tomorrow night. Perhaps by tonight, seeing as they couldn't keep their hands off each other. Obviously, I was forgotten. I guess, just because we arrived together, it didn't mean we would be leaving together. It wasn't as if Rio was looking around, wondering where I'd got to. He was enjoying the new bloke's attention too much.

Turning away from the sight of my sometimes-sort-of-boyfriend getting it on with another guy, I stomped over to the bar.

"Give me a Scotch. Neat."

"Um..." the pimple-faced youth behind the bar said hesitantly, looking like a rabbit caught in the headlights.

That was it. A simple 'um' and then he stood gawping at me like a brainless idiot. Whatever his problem was, I didn't give a shit. I also didn't see a drink coming my way.

"Um what?" I scowled at him.

"I'm sorry, but Mr. Darke said..."

"Not to serve me alcohol, right?"

The kid nodded miserably, and his eyes darted around the room, desperately seeking back up. Too bad for him, Rio was pre-occupied with eye-fucking his new roadie and wasn't likely to notice what I was up to. That's if they hadn't moved on to actual fucking in the nearest coat cupboard by now. I refused to turn my head and look.

"Okay, here's the deal." I said, my voice dripping with ice. "Rio Darke is a wanker, and he is not the boss of me. I'm a grown man and perfectly capable of making my own decisions. So, if I say get me a drink, you get me a fucking drink. Clear?"

"Yes, Sir. I'm sorry."

"And make it a double," I called after him as he scurried away.

I was even madder at Rio now. Who the fuck did he think he was, ordering the bar staff not to serve me alcohol? Not my boyfriend, evidently, or he wouldn't be making out with someone else right under my nose. I was mad at Mal too, for pointing out the obvious, and mad at the stupid pills for not working.

A drink arrived in front of me. I snatched up the glass, downing the amber liquid in one swallow. It burned my throat, but I welcomed the momentary discomfort, because there it was... that instant hit that took the edge off my misery. The warm, comforting glow within that made the world bearable.

"Another."

I banged the glass on the counter, harder than I meant to. It shattered in my hand, slivers of glass piercing my skin.

"I don't think –"

"Yeah, well lucky for you, you're not paid to think. You're paid to pour the fucking drinks, so get on with it."

The contents of the second glass went down the same way as the first. Finally, things were starting to get nice and hazy. Another glass, and I wouldn't care that Rio had betrayed me. Two more, and I wouldn't give a shit that he didn't love me. Fuck knows how many doubles it would take before I could forget how much I loved him.

"Garrison."

And there he was. The man of the hour. Creeping up behind me, while Spotty the bartender was pouring my third drink. I turned to face him, reminding myself the concern in his eyes was not genuine. The only person Rio Darke cared about was Rio Darke.

"Finished already?" I sneered. "That was quick, even for you."

Rio's jaw tightened, but he didn't deny getting jiggy with his little roadie friend.

"How many have you had?" he asked sternly, like it was any of his fucking business.

"Only one." I smirked and raised my middle finger, then gave him the reverse V. "Might have been two."

"It was two," the barman supplied helpfully. "They were doubles. I'm sorry, Mr. Darke."

"Alright, Spotty. Nobody asked you."

I should have known I couldn't trust the little rat. Didn't bartenders have to sign some sort of oath, like doctors, which prevented them from spilling all your dirty little secrets to any fucker that asked? The hypocritical oath. That was it.

"That's enough," Rio snapped. "You're causing a scene and you're embarrassing me."

"You embarrass yourself," I retorted. People had stopped what they were doing and were watching us. I didn't give a toss. If it was a free show they wanted, I was happy to give them one. "You think you're all that, Rio, but you're not. You're a joke. Literally a fucking joke. How do you tell when the stage is level? The drummer drools from both sides of his mouth. See? A joke! Do you even count as a real musician, Rio?"

"Stop," he said. "Come on. I'm taking you home."

He grabbed hold of my arm and the red mist descended. I shoved him hard, and he staggered backward, his face a mask of fury and shock.

"Fuck you!" I yelled. "Why don't you take your roadie bum-chum home instead?"

"Okay." Rio took a deep breath to steady himself. "Okay, Garrison. Have it your own way, just like you always do."

He pulled his phone from his pocket, not looking at me as he scrolled through his contact list. I didn't need to ask who he was calling. It made me sick, the way he and Dane thought they could pass me back and forwards, fighting over who got custody, because – God forbid – they left me to take care of myself.

"You want him, come and get him," Rio spat coldly into his phone. "I'm done."

"You're done? Maybe I'm done with you. How do you like that?" I put both my hands on his chest and shoved him again. "I, Am. Done. With. You."

Rio's laugh was entirely devoid of humour.

"Good."

I don't know what happened next. I didn't plan it. Wasn't even aware that my hands had formed into fists. Suddenly, everyone was shouting. Hands were grabbing at me and hustling me away, and Rio was on the floor, blood pouring between the fingers that covered his face. As I was dragged from the room, all I could do was look back over my shoulder and wonder how the hell he got there.

# Chapter Eighteen

"GARRISON, YOU NEED TO GET UP."

Dane's voice. As usual he managed to sound like he was my old man, and I was in trouble again. I tugged the quilt over my head and grunted like the sullen teen he treated me as.

"Go away. I'm sleeping."

"You've slept all day," Dane said impatiently. "It's gone three in the afternoon."

"Don't care. I'm tired, my headaches and my hand hurts." I rolled onto my back, peeking at him over the edge of the duvet. "Why does my hand hurt? What did I punch this time?"

Christ, I must have been on one hell of a bender last night. I didn't remember anything much. It wasn't the first time I'd woken up from a drinking session with a broken bone in my hand, though. I'd been known to punch walls before now, even the odd car or two if the urge took me.

"You don't remember?"

"Would I be asking if I did?"

"Seriously? There's nothing?" Dane asked dryly. He folded his arms and leaned on the door frame, waiting.

I frowned, screwing my face up in concentration. Apart from a banging headache, I didn't hurt any place other than my hand, so it was doubtful anyone had hit me. My lips curved into a lazy smile. There was one thing I could quite recall quite clearly.

"Rio looked hot as fuck."

Dane pushed himself upright and scowled.

"Get up, Garrison. We need to talk."

Turning on his heel, he strode out of the room. I didn't get why he was so pissed. I mean, okay, I fell of the wagon. It was hardly the first time. He clearly had to come and scrape my drunken arse out of the gutter – again, not for the first time – and put me to bed. What did he expect? I was a fall-down fucking drunk and Rio leaving was one of my biggest triggers. Dane was aware of both those facts.

Something about the night before tugged at the edge of my hazy memory. Whatever it was, it had my gut churning with anxiety. And the sudden nauseating feeling I had? I had a nasty suspicion it was nothing to do with my mega hangover. I flexed my bruised fingers in front of my face, wracking my brains as to how I managed to injure my hand. *What the fuck did I punch this time?* That was what I asked Dane. Maybe the real question was not what but *who*.

No. There was no way in Hell I would hit Rio. I loved him. I'd never do anything to physically hurt him. My imagination was running riot because I couldn't remember. That's all this was.

Then why did I feel so damn guilty?

I pushed back the duvet and leapt out of bed. My head spun and I had to take a moment to steady myself against the dresser. I needed a piss desperately and a shower wouldn't go amiss, but they would have to wait. Answers were what I needed more than anything and Dane had them.

Dane had taken the time to undress me before throwing my pathetic arse into bed, although he obviously stopped short of caring if I froze to death as he left me butt naked. Hands shaking – more in trepidation at learning the truth of my actions from the night before than any other reason – I pulled on a pair of boxer shorts and a t-shirt.

On wobbly legs, I slowly made my way down the stairs and through the vast house in search of Dane. I found him in the new, all mod-con kitchen with Riley. The younger man shot me a withering look before turning his attention back to the hot drinks he was in the middle of making. Whatever ground I'd gained with him in recent weeks, seemed to have been lost again in the wake of yesterday's events.

"Sit." Dane pointed to one of the stools at the breakfast bar.

I did as I was told and sat, like a good little dog. Usually, I would argue for the sake of it when he spoke to me in that tone of voice, but I didn't have the energy. Plus, Dane was the one with the answers I wanted, so starting a fight with him would be counterproductive.

Dane lowered his massive frame onto the stool beside me. Riley placed two steaming mugs in front of us, and I was surprised to smell the rich aroma of hot chocolate, my go-to beverage when I needed comforting. I didn't think Riley cared enough to make it for me. Although, he evidently didn't care enough to add whipped cream and marshmallows like Rio would have done. I'd probably be pushing my luck if I asked for them, so I thanked him and looked at Dane expectantly.

"Go on then, tell me."

"You really don't remember?"

I shrugged, displaying a nonchalance I really didn't feel. My attitude was hardly likely to endear me to Dane and Riley, but there were some guards it was impossible to drop, even in front of my best friend.

"I thought we already established that I don't."

Riley snorted in disbelief. "You don't remember going to a party you weren't invited to and getting off your face on drink and drugs? How convenient for you."

"How the fuck is not remembering shit convenient?" I retorted.

It wasn't like I was *choosing* to forget. And now that Riley mentioned drugs, I had a vague recollection of Mal offering me a baggie of white powder in the bathroom. I hadn't accepted, but I'd taken pills, hadn't I? Oxy. An image flashed into my mind., of standing at the sink and swallowing a handful of pills. Christ, no wonder I felt like shit. Alcohol on top of Oxy was a recipe for disaster.

Deciding to ignore Riley, I turned back to Dane.

"So, I got drunk and high, it's hardly the crime of the century. Anything else I should know about?"

"You mean other than punching your boyfriend in the face?" Riley asked scornfully.

"Oh, fuck off. I did no such thing!"

Except the ache in my hand was testament to the fact I'd hit something. I didn't want to believe it, but deep down I knew Riley was telling the truth. In my mind, I saw Rio lying on the floor, and me looking at him, wondering how he got there. Had I really struck him hard enough to knock him off his feet? I glanced at Dane, seeking confirmation. He nodded, the expression in his eyes deadly serious.

"You broke his nose, Garrison. It's a good job he's the drummer and not the lead singer."

"No, I..." I floundered helplessly, unable to deny what I was hearing. Rio was never going to forgive me. Not only had I hit him, but I'd humiliated him in front of his friends. I patted my hands down my body, although I was aware I didn't have any pockets in the scant clothing I wore. "Where's my phone? I need to call him. If I can just explain..."

Yeah, and how was I supposed to explain shit to anybody when I couldn't explain it to myself? I had no memory of punching him or the events leading up to that moment.

"Forget it," Dane said sharply, slipping into his habitual paternal role again. "Rio's gone. He'll be halfway across the Atlantic by now."

"He'll have his phone on him, though. If I..."

"Garrison, he doesn't want to hear from you," Dane told me, sounding a whole lot more sympathetic than I deserved in the circumstances. "He's blocked your number, so you can't contact him anyway. Cage and the other guys have too."

"Well, then you phone him and..."

"They blocked me too. I told them too, because I knew you'd try ringing him from my phone."

"No!" I exploded, leaping to my feet. Thankfully, my legs seemed a little steadier now, so I was spared the added embarrassment of falling on my arse. "He can't do this to me."

"I think you'll find you did it to yourself," Riley said smugly.

I glared at him, because if anyone deserved a smack in the face it was my best friend's boyfriend. Apparently, I did possess some small degree of common sense, because I managed to resist the urge to pound on his pretty little face until he was unrecognisable. Dane would pulverise me if ever dared to lay a finger on his precious boytoy.

Riley nudged Dane's arm. The little shit was enjoying my fall from grace way too much. It was probably all his idea to have everyone block both me and Dane, so I had no means of contacting Rio.

"Tell him the rest."

"Not now, Riley," Dane said abruptly.

"Yes, now," I interjected, because, honestly, how much worse could it get? Even if Rio pressed assault charges, I didn't have it in me to care. It was no more than I deserved after hurting the one person I was supposed to love more than anything. Riley was right about one thing. I'd brought this whole shitty situation down on my own head. The weight of my guilt was already crushing me, so what difference would a little more make? "What else did I do? And don't tell me I tried it on with Riley. There's not enough drugs and alcohol in the world to make me fancy his scrawny arse."

Riley pulled a face and I smirked. It was a cheap shot, but I wasn't about to sit back and let him have all the fun, however wrong my behaviour had been lately.

"You think you'd still be standing if you did?" Dane scoffed. "Just give it a rest, both of you."

He puffed out his chest and fixed each of us with a stern look, as if he was trying to assert his authority.

Because, yeah, like that was going to work on me or Riley. We might both love him in our separate ways, but each of us could run rings around him if we wanted to.

"You didn't just break Rio's nose," Riley said with a trace of smugness, ignoring Dane's low growl of warning. "You broke his heart. He loved you and you shit all over it."

Loved. Past tense. I wasn't going to take Riley's word for it, though. He and Rio had never been close, so it was unlikely Rio would ever confide him. If anyone had an insight into Rio's emotions and private thoughts, it would be Dane. Not me. Dane. I knew he and Rio talked, even if Dane didn't entirely approve of our relationship.

"That's bullshit, anyway," I retorted. "Rio doesn't love me. He said he did, but it wasn't true, was it? If he loved me, why would he leave me?"

Dane sighed heavily. He didn't want to have this conversation, but tough shit. Riley had kind of forced his hand, and I had a right to know what Rio told him about me.

"He wasn't leaving you."

I blinked at Dane, bewildered. Was I missing something here? Some big secret that I was the only one not privy to?

"Uh, hello... in case you didn't get the memo, he was already getting on a plane and going to another country for eight months before I hit him. How can that be construed as anything but leaving?"

"Because, you idiot, he was taking you with him!"

"What?" Okay, now I was beyond confused. We'd said our good-byes. Not once had Rio mentioned taking me on tour with him. In fact, he was adamant it wasn't even an option. "No, you're wrong. You must be. He would have said something."

"He wanted to surprise you," Dane continued. "He couldn't take you from the start, and he knew you'd sink into a depression once he'd gone, so he gave me an airline ticket for you to join him in New York in a couple of weeks. We thought it would cheer you up."

"And you agreed?" I questioned, finding it hard to believe Dane would let me go willingly. "What about recording the new album?"

"Listen, Rio came to me a few days ago and basically asked for my blessing. He told me he was in love with you and wanted you with him in America. He swore he would help you stay clean and sober. How could I refuse when I know being with him is all you want?" Dane shook his head despondently. "I was prepared to let you off the hook with making the album, but I guess that's redundant now. Rio told me to lose the ticket."

"And have you? Lost it, I mean?"

"No, not yet, but I'm not giving it to you."

I smiled coldly. "You realise I can just buy my own ticket and go to New York anyway?"

"Yes, but you won't," Dane said evenly. "You say you love Rio, so prove it. If you really love him... you'll let him go."

# Chapter Nineteen

"GO AWAY."

I was suffering from a serious case of déjà vu. Every morning, Dane appeared in my room and demanded I get out of bed. And every morning, I told him to fuck off and leave me alone. The routine became boring after the first couple of days. If I had the energy to care about anything whatsoever, I might have found it surprising that Dane hadn't given up on me yet. But no. Dane was as regular as clockwork, checking I was still alive and making me eat so that I stayed that way.

"It's been two weeks," Dane said patiently. "It's time for you to join the land of the living again."

"I'm fine where I am, thanks."

"Then I would say your definition of the word fine is highly questionable. I thought you were letting go."

Yeah, like it was that easy. Like I could just flip a switch in my heart and not love Rio anymore. If someone offered me a pill to wipe all my memories of the man, I would swallow it in a heartbeat and be done with it. It wasn't as though I *wanted* to feel the way I did.

"I still love him," I said miserably,

"I know you do, and God knows I love you too, Garrison, but the truth is, Rio deserves better."

Ouch, why not say it as it is? That was one sure-fire way to *not* cure my depression. Even my best friend saw me as a violent domestic abuser and thought the love of my life would be better off without me.

"Look," Dane began, his tone doubtful, as though he fully expected me to say no. "It's Jaded Intent's first studio session for the new album today. I was really hoping you'd come play with us, like you promised."

Something alien sparked in my chest, a faint glimmer of interest. I'd always been able to lose myself in music and maybe that was just what I needed. Not that I'd rehearsed any of the new songs, but I prided myself on being a quick learner. Call it a gift, but I pretty much only had to hear something once and I could play it faultlessly. A good, old jam session could be quite therapeutic, and rouse me from this funk I had fallen into. It wouldn't change my mind about leaving Jaded Intent, because Rio or no Rio, I didn't want to return to my old life. Much as I loved playing the guitar, I didn't need all the shit that came with being famous.

"What time are you planning on heading to the studio?" I asked, taking Dane by surprise. "Have I got time to shower and shave first?"

"We'll make time," Dane replied, looking immensely pleased that I'd agreed to do something other than lie in bed and stare at the ceiling, or search for articles about Rio online.

"I want to stop on the way and get my hair cut too," I told him, getting out of bed and running my fingers through the tangled and rapidly lengthening strands.

"You could always let it grow out again," Dane suggested lightly. "It suits you when it's longer."

I shook my head. "Rio likes it short."

Dane opened his mouth to argue and then closed it again. He knew which battles were not worth fighting. Persuading me out of bed and into the studio would have to be his win for the day.

Not that I was about to admit it to anyone, but it felt good to be washed, dressed and clean shaven. Dane was slightly scandalised when I chose to go to a bog-standard, high-street barber over his top-end hair stylist, but it was one more thing he would have to suck up and get over. The end result was the same, and I'd rather give ten quid to someone who deserved it, rather than pay two hundred to some pompous tit who didn't.

It was nice to see the others too, although KP seemed a bit stand-offish. In a whispered conversation, Dozer revealed that KP was still pissed at me for wanting to leave the band. They thought with Rio out of the picture, I would change my mind and stay. Which proved how little they understood. If they really believed Rio was my only reason for walking away from Jaded Intent, then they didn't know me at all. For once though, I was going to be an adult about it and not let them get to me. This was my final time playing with them and I was determined to go out on a high.

Late in the afternoon, we took a well-earned break and the guys ordered in food. I wasn't hungry, but I took a small plate of egg fried rice and sweet in Jack in just to keep Dane off my back. I sat on the floor in a corner of the studio, with a notepad balanced on my knee, and tuned out the inane chatter of my bandmates.

I didn't see Dane sneak up on me until the notebook was suddenly snatched away from my hand. He skimmed over the words, screwed crossed page in my untidy handwriting, and his eyes widened.

"Garrison, this is really good," he said, drawing the others to gather behind him and peer over his shoulder. "Have you got a melody in mind?"

"Sort of," I admitted reluctantly, because I could already see where this was heading. He was going to hate it when I told him no.

"Can you get it finished in time to go on the album?"

"Yes, but you can't have it." I held my handout for the notebook. "It's for Rio."

"Wait." Dane held the notebook out of my reach and scowled. "You promised to give us first refusal on anything you wrote."

"And I will," I said tiredly. Was that what he thought? That I was trying to curry favour with Rio by writing songs for Carnival, Jaded Intents biggest rivals? He didn't get it or me at all. "But not this one. This is Rio song."

"Fine." Dane tossed the notebook into my lap. "But don't think you can find him some sappy, little love song and he'll take you back. Life doesn't work that way."

"It might," I said.

# Chapter Twenty

**AFTER THE OTHERS** finished eating and I'd added a couple more lines to Rio song, the session resumed. Recording was not due to start until the next day, although they were sound engineers in the studio to check we sounded okay, and the producer called in briefly to speak to us. My smugness at being the only one not singled out for criticism didn't last long once Dozer reminded me that I'd slept with the guy a year or so back and he was hoping for a repeat performance. Which wasn't going to happen, because part of winning back Rio was proving I could be faithful, even when we were not together.

The guys thought I was kidding myself, but they didn't know Rio the way I did. Because, sure, he was angry and hurt at the moment, but he loved me. Giving Dane the plane ticket was proof that he wanted me. I was biding my time, giving him space to calm down and realise how much he missed me. Then we'd give this relationship thing another shot, and he'd appreciate the fact I hadn't slept with anyone else. My only hope was that he hadn't either. Under the circumstances, I guess I'd have to be willing to forgive and forget if he had. Him fucking someone else would make us even. I punched him in the face, and he punched me in the heart.

Just as we were preparing to call it a day, Dane's phone rang. He fumbled for it, embarrassed, while we all catcalled and jeered, because bringing a phone into the studio was a cardinal sin. Mine was still in the bedside cabinet. It wasn't like anyone other than Dane ever called it anyway, and I was in the same room as him pretty much twenty-four-seven lately.

Dane took the call outside and when he returned a few minutes later, his face was etched with worry.

"Riley's mum and dad were involved in a head-on car crash," he said. "They're alive, but critical. Come on, Garrison. We need to pick up Riley and get to the hospital."

I wasn't the only member of Jaded Intent who stared at him blankly, unable to comprehend the urgency. Most of us had troubled or non-existent relationships with our parents. Mine disowned me when I was nineteen and chose to be a musician rather than a dentist. KP's parents were divorced and moved on with new families, neither of them interested in the product of a marriage they'd rather forget. Dozer had grown up in foster care and was lucky to land on his feet at fifteen and placed with a family who were hugely supportive of his passion for music. Rio's parents were around somewhere, but he never went to visit and rarely spoke about them. Nobody knew the full story, but Cage had been raised by his grandmother from an early age. All we knew was, the guy had an almost pathological hatred for his mother. Even Dane got along better with his aunt and uncle than he did with his own parents. Riley was different, maybe because he wasn't famous or a musician.

"I'm not coming with you," I said, amazed he would even suggest it. "Riley won't want me there."

"I'm not leaving you by yourself."

"This isn't about me. It's about Riley. He needs you. I don't. If you love him as much as you say you do, you need to put him first for once." Look at me, pretending to be an adult and put someone else's problems before my own. "Don't throw away what you two have because of me, because if you choose me over him right now, he will never forgive you for it."

"I can't believe I'm saying this," KP jumped in, "but Garrison is right. Go take care of Riley. I'll make sure Garrison gets home in one piece."

"Go," I told Dane. "I'm not going to do anything stupid; I swear."

He gave me a doubtful look, probably because I'd demonstrated time and time again that our opinions on what defined stupid differed considerably.

"Fine," Dane said grudgingly. He wanted to rush off to be with Riley, not stand around argument with us. He pointed a thick finger in my direction. "But you, behave. And you..." The finger swivelled to KP. "You stay right be-fucking-side him until I get back."

KP nodded, although from the look he gave me, he was no more enamoured by the idea than I was. With that, Dane hustled out of the studio and with our lead singer gone, there was no point in the rest of us hanging around, so we left shortly after.

Conversation with KP on the way home was stilted and tense. We've been close not so long back, but KP didn't seem ready to forgive me for quitting the band. It was hard to understand why he wanted me around, when he'd been most vocal about staging an intervention and throwing my arse back into rehab. He was straight too, so it wasn't like he fancied me. Unless he secretly did, of course, which would explain why he was so resentful of Rio.

"You don't have to stay," I told him as we pulled up outside Dane's house. "I'm going straight to my room."

KP rolled his eyes. "Nice try. I don't like it any more than you do, but Dane said stay, so I'm staying."

"Hmmm, interesting."

"What is?" KP asked impatiently.

"Well, it's a given that Dane is the boss of me. I just wondered when he became the boss of you as well."

"He's not my boss, shithead." KP was irritated, which was what I set out to achieve. Pissing people off was kind of my forte, which was generally useful when I wanted them to leave me alone.

"And you're not my babysitter," I pointed out. "I'm going to bed and – unless you want to admit to having the hots for me – it would be pretty weird for you to come with me."

"I don't fancy you, Garrison."

"No, I know, I'm not saying you do, it's just... straight guys don't normally want to jump into bed with their gay friends."

I gave him an innocent smile before wetting my lip with the tip of my tongue.

"Okay, that's it. Get out of my car, Garrison."

"Don't you want to come in?" I teased. "We can fool around."

"Out!"

"Play hide the sausage..."

"Oh, my God, Garrison! Just go, will you."

I ran at the steps to the front door, laughing. KP shook his head as he drove away. Inside the hallway, the laughter died on my lips, and I sank to the floor with my back to the door. I was going to hell for this. So many lies. So much deceit. I was a terrible person and an even worse best friend.

But I couldn't stay sat there for long. I didn't know how much time I would have the house to myself for. Dan could be back at any moment with or without Riley. As soon as he realised I was not home and then learned I was not with KP, he would start searching. It would take his attention away from Riley, just when Riley needed him most. Riley would hate me more than he already did. KP would be mad because I tricked him. I needed to be gone before any before any of that happened. Like on a plane somewhere over the Atlantic.

Dragging myself from the floor, I headed to Dane's study. It would have been quicker and easier to buy my own ticket, but for some reason it was important I use the one Rio bought me. It was symbolic. In my gut, I knew Dane wouldn't have binned it. The ticket would be hidden somewhere in the house. I just had to find it.

The study was the obvious place to start. Deep down, I knew Dane would have more sense than to leave it lying around in the first place I would look. Then again, maybe he would try to double bluff me, and the study was exactly where he would hide it.

Moving as quickly as I could, I worked my way methodically around the room, then through draws and peering between each of the many books lining the bookshelves. The ticket was not there.

I bit my lip, questioning my next move. If Dane and Riley came home unexpectedly and caught me in their bedroom, they would be furious and rightly so. Not that they had ever specifically stated their room was out of bounds. It was more of a tacit understanding. But the trust they had that I would never breach their inner sanctum made it the perfect place to keep something they did not want me to see.

I hesitated momentarily on the threshold, knowing I was going a step too far. After everything I'd done, all this shit I'd pulled, I knew invading their privacy so blatantly would be the last straw. This was the one thing they would not find it in their hearts to forgive.

Then I went in anyway, because when it came down to it, I loved Rio more than I love Dane. More than I loved myself. I would deal with the consequences of my actions, whatever they may be, but the need to get to Rio, to sing him his song, was all consuming. In that moment, nothing else mattered. The room was tidy, much more so than mine. The bed was made and there were no clothes littering the floor. It had to be down to Riley, because I shared rooms with Dane on tour dozens of times and he'd never been a neat and house-proud type.

I pulled open the drawer in the bedside cabinet. Lube. Condoms. A silver butt-plug... I really didn't need to see that. Didn't want to imagine whose it was or where it had been. A wristwatch, a pen, a half empty packet of paracetamol. No paper that I could see though.

Going around the side of the bed, I open the door in the other bedside cabinet. More sex stuff. Jesus, how many times did these guys have sex? Even Rio and I were not that rampant. Well, we probably were but it was different. Dane and Riley were like an old married couple. They should be past the sex-at-every-opportunity stage.

Still, there was no ticket among the evidence of their vivacious sex life.

I made a slow circuit of the room, opening drawers and pushing socks, undies and folded T-shirts aside. Just as I was beginning to think I was conducting an exercise in futility and should just go to the airport and buy my own bloody ticket, I spotted it. The corner of an envelope sticking out from beneath a pair of Dane's boxer shorts. I grabbed it, hardly daring to breathe as I ripped open the envelope and pulled out an airline ticket with my name on it.

Stuffing it into my pocket, I hurried to my room and dragged out the overnight bag I'd stashed in the bottom of my wardrobe. It wasn't as though I could have anticipated something happening to Riley's parents, but I couldn't deny my bag had been packed, waiting for the opportune moment to make my escape. I truly hoped his mum and dad made it through okay, but I also kind of hoped Dane would be with them at the hospital for a few hours yet. The longer he was gone, the further away I would be by the time he discovered I was missing.

Like I said, I was not a good person.

I turned up the collar of my coat and jammed a beanie onto my head. I was pretty sure Dane had some psychic way of knowing when and where I went by Uber, so I would take a bus to the city, then jump on the Tube. Joe Public didn't know about my haircut yet, so it was unlikely I'd be recognised, but still, I preferred to reduce the risk as much as possible.

In the end, getting to the airport on public transport was surprisingly easy and nobody really paid me any attention. I was glad of it. I never been one of those rock stars who thrived on public adoration. Just the opposite, in fact.

Although, nor was I opposed to use my fame to get what I wanted. I did exactly that when I arrived in check-in hall. Waltzing confidently up to the desk and asking the handsome young man behind it to get me onto the first available flight to New York. It always helped when the person I was trying to sweet talk was a fan, and by the way the kid's eyes lit up when he saw me, he obviously was one. My gaydar happened to be pinging off the scale as well, so I added a little flirtation into mix to keep him keen. I had no intention of acting on it, of course. He was working and I was going to New York to win back the only man I ever loved, so no way was I blowing it by messing around with another guy.

Thankfully, batting my eyelashes, biting my bottom lip and flashing a few sexy Garrison smiles seemed to do the trick. Wonder of wonders, he found me a first-class seat on a flight scheduled to leave within the next hour. Maybe it was all down to the guy behind the desk, or maybe there was a God after all, but someone was certainly looking out for me. By the time Dane figured out what I was doing and could try to stop me, I'd be long gone. Even so, I was able to breathe a little easier once I was in my seat and the plane was coasting down the runway.

Chapter Twenty-One

LONDON WAS COLDER than a witch's tit when I left, but New York was on a whole other level. Positively Arctic. I shivered in my too-thin coat and beanie hat, which might as well be made of lace for all the protection it gave my poor ears. So, my first stop was to buy a New York proof coat, a proper hat with faux-fur lined earflaps and a pair of fleece-lined gloves.

More suitably attired, I set out for the venue where I knew Carnival were playing. By the time I got there the show would be almost over, but I wasn't there to see the band, only Rio. If I could get him alone when he came off stage, give him his song, he would forgive me for punching him. I knew he would.

I could hear the faint strain of rock music from outside the arena. People milled about at the entrance, security and fans leaving early to beat the mad rush when the concert ended. That wasn't my way in, though. It wouldn't get me to Rio, and while it seemed unlikely I would be recognised in my current attire, it was still a possibility. Carnival, I knew, tended to party in the dressing rooms after a show, but I didn't want anything to hold me up, preventing me from finding Rio before he left.

Heading around the side of building, I made my way to the rear, where rows of articulated trucks lined up, waiting to carry the stage equipment and lighting to the next venue, and limos waited to transport the band to whatever hotel they were staying in overnight. It shouldn't have been as easy to gain access to the area as it was, but I wasn't complaining as I slipped between two of the huge lorries.

Doing my best to look casual, I ambled across the asphalt to an open service door. I nearly made it too, before a guy – who made Dane looked like a prepubescent teenager in comparison – stepped into my path. He put a hand on my chest, although his size alone stopped me from going any further.

"You can't be back here."

"It's okay. I'm with the band."

"Sure you are." He jerked his thumb over his shoulder to where a half dozen roadies stood, ready to leap into action as soon as Carnival came off the stage. "How come you're not dressed the same as them?"

"I'm not part of the crew," I said. "I'm with Rio Darke."

"Sure you are."

"Seriously. Look, I'm Garrison."

I tore the hat from my head and ran a hand over my newly cropped hair, suddenly self-conscious. Right now, I didn't much resemble the man people were used to seeing on stage and television or in photos.

"Garrison Swann," I pressed, seeing his blank expression. "You know, from Jaded Intent."

The giant goon raised an eyebrow.

"Never heard of you."

"Really? You've never heard of Jaded Intent?" I echoed in disbelief. "How about Dane Black? Have you heard of him?"

"Hell, yeah. Who hasn't?"

The guy was messing with me. He had to be. How could he know who Dane was and not me?

Over the speakers, I could hear Cage's gravel-laden voice launch into their final song. The show was nearly over. Rio would be coming off stage at any moment and I needed to be there waiting for him. I wanted to be the first person I saw, to prove that I was there for him. That I had flown halfway across the world to prove my love for him. None of which was going to happen if this big lump of stupid didn't get out of my way.

"Osi, it's okay. Let him in. He's who he says he is."

I turned to see who had spoken from behind me, my face morphing into a scowl as I recognised the roadie who Rio had been canoodling with in the corner at Carnival's leaving party. He was the reason I started drinking in the first place that night and ended up decking Rio. He was the last person I wanted coming to my aid, but if he could get me inside, I was prepared to swallow my pride and accept it.

The oversized wall of flesh – apparently named Osi – stepped aside grudgingly and allowed the two of us to pass. The roadie, whose name I couldn't remember, or if Rio had ever told me what it was to begin with, led the way. He glanced over his shoulder as we walked, shooting me an anxious look.

"I'm not sure how pleased he'll be to see you," he warned.

"What? Does he talk to you about me?" I asked jealously.

Had Rio continued to see the guy after the party? Were they a thing now? No, that didn't add up. If he was Rio's new fuck-toy, he wouldn't be helping me. He'd want to keep me as far away from Rio as possible.

"To be honest," the roadie said, "Rio doesn't talk to anyone much. But I was there the last time you saw each other. I remember how it ended."

"Then why let me in?"

"Because whatever you might think of me, I'm a decent guy. I'm not trying to steal your man. I have one of my own at home, thank you very much. Besides, there would no point chasing Rio. not when he's obviously still pining after you." He stopped outside a dressing room door and hesitated, his hand resting lightly on the handle. "I'm a sucker for a love story, okay? If you two can kiss and make up, we all get a happy ending."

Despite my churning gut and racing heart, I laughed.

"You're risking your job and breaking me into Rio's dressing room just so you can witness someone else's happy-ever-after? Are you for real?"

"You're the one taking all the risk," he said with a smirk. "Rio's not the only one in this dressing room. Cage is as well." he threw the door open and ushered me inside. "If Rio doesn't kill you on sight, Cage will probably do it for him."

He walked away, chuckling to himself as the door swung shot behind him. Maybe he wasn't as much of a decent guy as he claimed to be. Not if he was going to stand back and let Cage do the dirty work, while he swooped in and picked up the pieces of Rio's broken heart in the aftermath.

The dressing room was unmistakeably Rio and Cage's. Their clothes were strewn everywhere, making it look as though they'd moved in permanently, rather than for just one night. I suspected more than a fair share of the mess belonged to Cage, because Rio was never this untidy at home. *Home.* I guess that was a poor choice of words in the circumstances. If my song failed to win Rio back, chances were I'd never share his home again. I wouldn't even have a home, because staying at Dane's forever was not a viable option.

I picked up a battered, old acoustic guitar and began to idly strum the strings. I knew it belonged to Cage, although he only ever played it in private. Despite his role as Carnival's frontman, he had a strange aversion to playing his guitar before an audience. Admittedly, he wasn't as good as me, or even Boone, but he didn't totally suck either.

Music was coming through the speakers now that was not live from Carnival. Ironically, the track currently playing was a Jaded Intent one. Maybe it was a deliberate ploy to empty out the arena as quickly as possible. Our respective fans tended to be loyal and dislike the other band on principal.

I braced myself. Rio and Cage were going to burst through the door at any second. Neither was likely to be pleased to see me. And holding Cage's guitar in front of me like a shield was not about to do me any favours. Cage was bound to kick off if he found me touching his shit.

Cage was the first to barge his way into the room. On seeing me, he stopped so abruptly that Rio cannoned into the back of him. With a low growl of annoyance, Rio punched his lead singer's shoulder.

"What the fuck, Cage?"

"Your slut boyfriend is here."

"That's rich coming from you," I retorted. "Hypocrite much, Cage?"

"Piss off, Garrison. You're not wanted here." He smirked; confident Rio was going to back him up. "Leave the guitar."

"What for?" I snapped. "It's not like *you* can actually play it."

Cage took a step forward and I braced myself, knowing his tendency to let his fists do the talking whenever his brain couldn't form the necessary words. But then he stopped and looked round in surprise when Rio grabbed his arm.

"Give us five, eh, Cage?"

"What? No. I'm not leaving you alone with him."

"Nothing's going to happen. I want to talk to him. In private."

"And where am I supposed to go?" Cage demanded, shooting a furious look in my direction. "I just came off stage. I need to shower and put my normal clothes on."

"Go next door. Mal won't mind."

Mal would probably mind quite a lot, because although Carnival only walked off stage five minutes ago, if he was true to form, he would be snorting coke off a hooker's tits by now. Maybe even two hookers. Mal wasn't fussy at the best of times, let alone when he was on a post-gig high. Still, not my problem. Cage had to know the shit his bandmate got up to.

Muttering dire threats under his breath, Cage gathered up an armful of clothes and a washbag and stormed back out of the room. Which left me alone with Rio, who was still drenched in sweat from drumming all night. Not that I minded. I had nothing against a bit of sweat when it was honestly earned. He wasn't exactly welcoming though. He stood with his strong arms folded across his muscled chest, without even a glimmer of a smile. Something told me he wasn't pleased to see me, but then I used to that. He seldom was.

"What do you want, Garrison?"

"I... I just want to talk. To apologise in person for what I did. I was drunk. Completely wasted. I never would have hit you otherwise. You must know that."

He shrugged one shoulder and didn't answer. Damn it, he was going to make me work for his forgiveness. I was prepared to do whatever it took. Go down on bended knee and beg. Suck his dick while I was down there. I'd even swallow. Anything, so long as he gave me another chance.

"I... um... wrote you a song."

"A song?" Rio arched a sardonic eyebrow.

"Yeah, I... wait. Give me a sec."

I laid Cage's guitar on the small two-seater sofa and hurriedly stripped off my cumbersome coat and gloves. Picking up the guitar again, I hung the strap around my neck and lightly strummed the strings. Thankfully, it was in tune. This situation was painful enough without the instrument sounding shit. I could make myself sound bad without any help. Guitarist extraordinaire and master songwriter I may be, but I was sadly lacking in the singing department.

"Can I play it for you?" I looked at him hopefully.

So far, he hadn't budged an inch. He maintained his stance, arms folded, feet apart, his expression cold enough to freeze molten lava. It felt like an eternity before he gave a grudging nod.

"Okay, but just remember I'm not a singer. And I haven't sung this out loud yet. I mean, I know how I want it to sound in my head but–"

"For fuck's sake, Garrison. I just came off stage. I'm tired. I'm sweaty, I stink, and I'm not in a good mood. Don't make it worse by pissing me off."

"Okay, sorry. Here goes..."

I took a deep breath and began to play, letting the melody wash over me before I started to sing.


*YOU SAY YOU CAN'T BE MY HAPPINESS*
  *You know it's not all that you are*
  *You are the air that I breathe*
  *My life. My soul. My heart*
  *You are my reason for living*
  *You are the reason I wake*
  *You are the guiding light in my darkness*
  *You are every good decision I make*
  *You say you can't be my happiness*
  *But without you I'm not happy at all*

*Because you are the only one I can love*
*The one who catches me whenever I fall...*


I stopped playing and was met by awkward silence.

"That's kind of all I've got for now. It needs work."

"Thank you," he said eventually. "It's a nice song and I appreciate the sentiment, but..."

"But what?"

"But you need to go home, Garrison. I love you, but I can't be with you. Not when I can't trust you. You hurt me, and not just physically. A pretty song isn't going to change any of that."

# Chapter Twenty-Two

I PUT Cage's guitar back on its stand and left. What else could I do when Rio made it abundantly clear he didn't want me there? I pleaded my case and I lost. Rio was never going to forgive me, so what did I do now? Slink home with my tail between my legs and try to carry on? Did I go back to the band and the only life I'd known since I was eighteen? Or did I buy my cottage beside the sea and leave everything – Rio included – behind me? Fucked if I knew the way forward. At that precise moment in time, there was no way I could envisage any sort of future without Rio.

Once I was outside in the busy corridor, which was full of people flying in every direction, I realised I'd forgotten to pick up my coat, hat and gloves. Now I was doubly fucked. I didn't want to go back into the dressing room and retrieve them. Not while Rio was in there. But I couldn't leave without them either, unless I wanted to die from hypothermia before I reached the end of the street.

Glancing around, I hoped someone would stop and help. Offer to go in and get them for me. But this wasn't my show, and I wasn't the biggest star in the building. Nobody paid me any attention, all of them too busy rushing around and caught up in their own business to even notice me.

A door opened close to where I stood and Cage and Mal stepped into the corridor, their body language angry and determined. I ducked into a stairwell before they spotted me. My guess was, it was my presence that had them all riled up, and they were on their way to rescue Rio from my villainous clutches. Cage had his own special way of dealing with problems and I doubted he cared about going back to prison so long as he got me out of Rio's life. If he had Mal as back-up, it would be best if I avoided them for the sake of my health.

Without thinking, I began to climb the stairs. I had no goal in mind other than escape the sting of Rio's rejection, as well as stay beyond the reach of a furious Cage's retribution. As ridiculous as it sounded, I was almost surprised to find myself on the roof of the arena, as if I hadn't figured out that was where the stairs would lead me.

A bitter wind lashed my body, so cold it felt as though the skin was being flayed from my cheeks. Regardless, I stumbled out onto the roof, my heart as cold and numb as my face and hands. I tucked my hands into my armpits in a vain attempt to warm them. Strong gusts buffeted me sideways, but I possessed neither the sense nor desire to turn around and go back inside. Instead, I battled my way forward, striving to reach the low parapet that ran around the edge of the roof.

Even shrouded in darkness, the view was breathtakingly beautiful. Thousands upon thousands of twinkling lights as far as the eye could see. Some stretching into the night sky and others moving in straight lines at street level. Far below me, I could see the last dregs of Carnival fans, as small as ants as they left the arena and wound their ways back to their cars and buses, or to the subway station. Thinking how these people had homes and families and lovers waiting for them made me feel sad. Sad and lonely. Most of them would probably envy me, believing I had everything and never realising they were the lucky ones. Incapable of understanding that *they* had so much more than me. Their lives were full. They mattered. My life was empty and meaningless.

It wasn't fair to lay the responsibility for my continued existence at Rio's door, but I needed him. Without him, I was nothing and nobody.

And now, here I was again. Literally on the precipice. Did I try and carry on? Build a life for myself that didn't revolve around Rio? Did I even want to? Or was it easier to give up? Surrender my soul to the inevitable? Because, let's face it, my death had been a long time coming. I should have overdosed or died from alcohol poisoning years ago, but my stubborn-ass body refused to stop living, even when there was nothing left to live for. So maybe it was time to take the choice away from my body and let fate decide instead. It wouldn't be hard. All I had to do was climb onto the parapet and let the wind blow me over the side. I wouldn't even have to jump.

The result would be the same. Me splattered all over the asphalt and Rio guilty ridden for the rest of his life. Was that really what I wanted? For Rio to blame himself and regret sending me away? If I wasn't around to see it, what did it matter what he or anyone else thought or felt, or who was held accountable?

I placed one foot on the parapet and wobbled, instantly unbalanced by the relentless and unforgiving wind. One more step and it could all be over...

"Garrison, stop!"

I turned my head, the stinging wind causing my eyes to water uncontrollably. Even though my vision was blurred, I knew who was on the roof with me. Sweet Ricky Boone. His band, Original Sin, were the support act for Carnival. I'd almost forgotten that. Boone and his guys were lucky. They started out as a Jaded Intent tribute band, which was okay for CJ, the band's lead singer and Boone's boyfriend. He was Dane's cousin and looked and sounded exactly like him. Boone was supposed to be me, although he was short and blond and bore no resemblance to me whatsoever. The kid played a mean guitar though. They'd had their problems in the beginning, including Boone spending time in rehab. But they'd also been incredibly fortunate, hitting the big time after playing only a handful of gigs. They hadn't had to work at it for years like the rest of us.

Boone wore a denim jacket, which was woefully inadequate for standing on a rooftop in a howling gale, but then when he donned it, I don't suppose the roof was where he imagined he was heading. His blond hair whipped around his face, and he clung to a vertical metal pole with both hands. It was a wise move. There was next to nothing of the guy. The wind would scoop him up and toss him over the edge in the blink of an eye.

"What are you doing?" I had to shout to make myself heard. "It's dangerous out here."

"No shit, Sherlock," he bellowed back. "I followed you. What are *you* doing?"

I wasn't sure how I should respond. Saying I was avoiding Cage and Mal was an honest answer, but it didn't explain why I was doing a death-defying balancing act on the edge of the arena roof. Of course, telling him I was contemplating chucking myself off was being truthful as well. Not jumping, exactly. If I stood on the parapet and let what happened happen, that didn't count as suicide. It was purely a matter of fate. Either way, I wouldn't be leaving anyone behind who cared. I did feel kind of bad about doing it in front of Boone, though. The kid was already fucked up, without me adding to it.

"I'm just admiring the view," I said, which wasn't a complete lie because I had been struck by the beauty of the city lights when I saw them.

"Do you think you could admire it a bit further away from the edge?" Boone asked. "Or even better... at ground level?"

"Wouldn't be the same."

"Even so... you wouldn't want to fall over by accident."

The *"or would you?"* went unsaid, but I could hear it in his voice. See it written all over his face. Boone thought I came up here to kill myself, but he was wrong. Letting nature take its course was not the same as being suicidal. I wasn't choosing to die. I was just seeing what happened. For all I knew, the wind would blow me back onto the roof and, if that was the case, I would accept that too. Take it as a sign this was not my time to go.

"Garrison, I've been where you are," Boone continued, which was funny really because he had to be at least a decade younger than me. Whatever bad place he assumed me to be in mentally, I was pretty sure I'd been there, done that and bought the t-shirt long before him. "I know how you feel. I know what it's like to not see a way forward. To think nobody cares if you live or die."

I snorted, although I doubted he heard it across the divide between us. "Difference being, you had CJ."

"And you've got Dane."

"No, Dane belongs to Riley." I shook my head. It had never been like that between me and Dane anyway. We were best friends. Brothers. "He'll be better off without me. All I do is mess everything up for him."

Well, shit. Even to my own ears, it sounded an awful like I'd made my mind up to end things. When did that happen? When had I subconsciously decided to jump? Meaning all this leaving-it-to-fate mumbo-jumbo was bullshit.

"What about Rio?" Boone asked, still clinging to the metal pole. "He loves you."

"He doesn't, though. Not really." I smiled sadly, only just realising the truth of it. "He says he does, but he doesn't mean it. He does it so I look like the arsehole in this relationship and he's a victim."

"So... what? Do you really want to die? Or do you just want to punish Rio for not loving you enough?"

I turned away from Boone, staring out across the city streets. The tears in my ears were no longer caused by the merciless wind. They came from the pain of my heart breaking all over again. Rio didn't love me enough. Thank you, Boone, for pointing it out to me. It wasn't as if I didn't already know, but still...

And maybe, not all that deep down, I did want to punish Rio. I wanted him to suffer. To know that *he* had brought about my untimely demise. In all likelihood, he wouldn't be upset about it for too long. One week. Two, if I was lucky. And I wouldn't be around to see it anyway, which made offing myself to spite someone else seem pointless. What was it I said to Rio when we were at the cottage? *I don't want to die. I'm just not sure I want to live either.* Something along those lines. I felt the same way now. It was hard to care one way or the other, yet I still couldn't bring myself to take that final step into oblivion.

Suddenly, big strong arms circled my waist and yanked me backwards, away from the edge. I yelped in surprise and outrage as I hit the ground with a resounding thud. My assailant rolled on top of me, pinning me down as though he expected me to try and break free and sprint to my death.

He was a big bastard; I'd give him that. If I don't know better, I'd swear it was Dane. But Dane was on another continent, and unaware of my current location. It couldn't be him. Besides, I'd been his friend long enough to know the difference between Dane and his near-identical cousin.

"What the fuck, CJ?" I ground out furiously, pushing at his chest. Yeah, like I had any realistic hope of dislodging the great oaf.

"Is that Garrison-speak for thank you?" his gravelly voice drawled in my ear. "I did just save your life, after all."

"Why would I thank you for that?" I meant to scoff at him, but my words came out as more of a broken sob. "Did I ask you to save me?"

"No, but I risked my life to do it and so did Boone."

CJ jerked his head towards his boyfriend.

"Well, then... *thank you.*" I injected as much sarcasm into my voice as I could manage. "You did a great job. Never saw you coming. Now, will you get the fuck off me?"

"Not yet."

"What the hell does that mean?" I wriggled underneath him, but he didn't budge an inch. "Look, I'm not going to do anything stupid. Just let me up."

"No."

Okay, I didn't want to resort to violence, but he kind of forced me into it. I slipped a hand between our bodies and grabbed a handful of nuts. CJ's whole body stiffened, but instead of jumping off me, he laughed. Actually laughed. Like the fact I literally had him by the short and curlies, amused him.

"If I let you up, I hope you can run fast," he said, his lips against my ear. "Because Boone doesn't share, and when he sees what you've got hold of, he'll rip you to fucking shreds with his bare hands."

"I'm bigger than he is. I'm sure I'll be okay."

"He's small," CJ agreed, "but he's vicious. Like a little terrier. And you're touching his bone."

I let go. CJ wasn't bothered in the slightest that I had him by the nutsack, which made me think his balls must be made of steel. How could he not find it painful, for fuck's sake? Boone, on the other hand, was likely to object strongly, if CJ was to be believed. Death by oblivion was one thing. Death by Boone would be a whole different ball game. No pun intended.

"So, are we just going to lie here until we catch pneumonia?" I asked sourly, annoyed with myself as much as CJ. It was stupid of me not to realise he would be there. He and Boone were practically joined at the hip. Where one went the other followed. Obviously, Boone had been deployed as the decoy and I was too dumb to notice his big, meathead boyfriend sneaking up on me. "Seriously, man, what are we waiting for?"

"Them," CJ answered.

He leapt to his feet with surprising agility for a man of his size and pulled me up with him. His grip was tight around my bicep. CJ dragged me across the rooftop towards the door where Boone waited with four other men. Two were dressed in arena security staff uniforms. The other two were cops. Security, I could understand, but the cops? Why were they involved? Last I heard, it wasn't illegal to stop and admire the view.

"What you did was dangerous," one of the cops complained when we reached them, and it took me a moment to realise he was addressing CJ and not me. "You should have waited for us."

"And you should have been here sooner," CJ retorted. Like his cousin, he wasn't one to back down, even from the law. "Still, if I'd waited, you wouldn't have had to climb all those stairs. You could have just scraped him up from the car park."

"I wasn't going to jump," I pointed out. Not that anyone was listening to me. Or if they were, they didn't believe me. Which was fair enough. I didn't entirely believe me either.

*No!* I wasn't going to jump. I was going to let the wind take me, which was different. It couldn't be deemed a suicide attempt when I'd left it to the fates to decide whether I lived or died.

I was frog-marched down the stairs in the middle of the six of them. At the bottom, the police officers took me off CJ's hands. Slowly, it dawned on me that they were taking me into custody for my own safety, which was ridiculous. I wasn't going to hurt myself. If fate had chosen to let me live for now, who was I to argue? I heard the words *psych evaluation* and balked. No fucking way! I wasn't going to jump. They couldn't lock me up for something I didn't do.

CJ's mammoth presence at my back compelled me to keep moving forward with the cops. We spilled into the corridor, and I was mortified to see how many people lined the walls to witness my walk of shame.

Carnival stood together in their entirety, arms folded across chests and faces like stone. Rio was strategically placed in their centre, a deliberate move by the others to show they were protecting him from the crazy ex.

"Rio, I wasn't going to jump," I pleaded as we drew level. "Please, you have to tell them. Tell them I'm not suicidal."

Rio took a step forward, despite Cage's effort to stop him. For a brief moment, I thought he was going to do it. He was going to defend me and make all of this go away.

He didn't.

"Do you know how sick I am of hearing the same old bullshit?" he asked coldly. "*I didn't mean it. I wasn't going to. I would never...* You keep doing this to me, Garrison. You keep lying and I... I just can't. Not anymore."

He turned on his heel and strode away, the rest of the band scurrying after him like the rats they truly were. I gave up the fight. Allowed the cops to lead me outside and put me into the back of their car. Boone pressed his hand to the glass and gave me a weak smile. Behind him, CJ was on his phone, probably giving Dane a blow-by-blow account of what I'd done to embarrass him and Jaded Intent's reputation this time.

I leaned my head against the glass and closed my eyes. Rio was right about me. I was a liar.

Because I wished whole heartedly that I'd jumped while I had the chance.

# Chapter Twenty-Three

PACING around my small private room like a caged animal, I was beside myself with rage. Literally fuming. If there wasn't smoke pouring from my ears, there damn well ought to be. They fucking sectioned me. *Me!* Garrison fucking Swann. Thrown in the nuthouse along with a whole load of genuinely crazy losers. On my way to my room, I'd seen a guy shit in his own hand and eat it, shouting all the while about it being the only way to stop the government stealing it from him. Then there was the middle-aged woman who sat in the corner and cried incessantly. I didn't know her story, but the constant wailing was getting on my last nerve. How could anyone think I belonged with these people?

The only saving grace was I had my own room. Oh, the perks of being rich and famous. Go me. The sad truth was it resembled a prison cell more than a private hospital suite. There were bars on the window, for fuck's sake.

The staff had politely refused my request to make a phone call. It wasn't an automatic right, apparently, as I hadn't been arrested. I begged to differ on that score because it sure as hell seemed to me as though I had been. I was confident in my belief that nobody here was under the illusion my stay was voluntary.

It didn't matter in the long run. Who did I have to call anyway? Rio would hang up the second he heard my voice, and Dane was in England taking care of his boyfriend. It didn't take a genius to figure out international calls were going to be a big no-no anyway. I didn't have CJ's number, and even if I did, what was I going to say? *Thanks for nothing, douchebag.*

The nurses wanted me to sleep, which was never going to happen. I wasn't manic like the shit-eater and the crying lady, but I was too on edge to relax. Next, they wanted to shove a shitload of meds down my throat. Also not happening. They threatened to tell the authorities my behaviour was irrational and uncooperative. I retaliated by threatening a lawsuit if they did anything against my will and they backed off, leaving me to stew in my room.

It was early afternoon when I was summoned to meet with the shrink appointed to my case. Andrea Mellor was a short dumpy woman, distinctly average in appearance, with thick rimmed spectacles and curly grey hair. Her clothes were long and floaty, a colourful array of pastels. I wondered if she always dressed that way, or if it was a deliberate ruse to convince her patients she was the maternal, hippy-chick type who could be trusted implicitly. Going by her soft drawl she was a Southern belle, although maybe the accent was as fake as the rest of her.

For a full fifteen minutes after I was ushered into her office, not a single word passed between us. She sat in a highbacked armchair, notepad and pen in her lap, and studied me as much as I did her.

Irritatingly, I was the first to crack under the weight of oppressive silence.

"You can't be much of a head doctor," I snapped, "if you don't ask any fucking questions."

She smiled, like I'd just complimented her outfit or something, not cussed her out.

"Ah, profanity," she said lightly. "The go to response of young men the world over. You realise, it shows a marked lack of intelligence, don't you? And you don't strike me as a stupid man, Mr Swann. Or may I call you Garrison?"

I scowled at her from my position on the couch. I wanted to get up and pace, but I wasn't sure if it was allowed. The brick shithouse orderly who'd escorted me here from my room had ordered me to sit. So, I sat.

Being a rule breaker at heart, it went against the grain to blindly obey anybody, but I didn't want the big goon coming back in and physically restraining me. I still had bruises forming from the previous night's encounter with CJ.

Staying put wouldn't stop me from running my mouth though. It was in my nature to rebel in some way.

"First of all, I'm in my thirties, so I'm not exactly young. Second, research proves that people who swear are generally smarter than those who don't. And you can call me whatever you want so long as it's a taxi to get me the fuck out of here."

Andrea smiled serenely and jotted something down in her notebook. I didn't bother asking what she'd written because I knew she wouldn't tell me.

"I see from your notes you're a musician," she said. "Have you done anything I might have heard of?"

"Are you shitting me? You sit there trying to get a rise out of me, and you don't even know who I am?"

"No, sorry. Should I?"

I laughed. "No, why the fuck would you? I'm nobody."

"We're all somebody," she said piously. I rolled my eyes and she noticed, marking another comment in her little book. "Does it annoy you when people don't know who you are, Garrison?"

"On the contrary," I replied. "Generally, I prefer it when they don't."

"You don't appreciate your fame?"

I shrugged, but that wasn't it. Not really. She made it sound as though I was ungrateful. Like I was undeserving of the career and the fortune I'd built for myself. She was wrong. I'd earned every accolade and every penny with blood, sweat and tears. A lot of tears at times, mainly behind closed doors where nobody could see. I wasn't ungrateful. Wanting a new life didn't mean I was unappreciative of the old one. Not when it had given me so much.

"Tell me about Rio," Andrea said when I didn't answer her previous question.

"What is there to say?" I sounded defensive, but so what? All of this was Rio's fault anyway. Whatever I said, she would make stupid, little notes in her stupid, little book and judge me. "We fucked. I messed up. He dumped me. End of."

"How did that make you feel? Were you angry with Rio for ending your relationship?"

"Of course, I was fucking angry!"

Andrea didn't flinch at my raised voice. She added a few more lines to her notes.

"Who were you trying to hurt by going up on that roof, Garrison? You or Rio?"

I paused. "Neither of us. I wasn't going to jump."

"That's not the impression you gave your friends," she said calmly.

"Yeah, well... they're wrong."

"They're worried about you."

"So?" I answered belligerently.

What difference did it make if CJ and Boone cared about me or not? CJ was Dane's cousin. I'd helped them out by performing in Boone's place when he was drugged and left for dead, but I didn't consider them to be my friends. I hardly knew them. It wasn't as if we played an integral part in each other's lives. I wasn't expecting an invite to their wedding if they were ever dumb enough to get married.

"I don't want to talk anymore." I leaned back on the cushion and folded my arms. "Can I go back to my cell?"

"You're not in prison, Garrison."

"No? Then how come it feels like I am? I mean, I can't leave if I want to, can I?"

"Not at the moment, no, but it's for your own safety." She sighed. "There's still time left in our session. I'd like to ask you a few more questions, if that's okay."

"Do what you like. You can't make me answer if I don't want to."

Great. Now I'd resorted to childish retorts. That was really going to convince them I was a rational, sane adult who was ready to be released back into the wild.

Tears of self-pity pricked my eyes. I didn't belong here. I didn't know where home was anymore, but that was where I wanted to be. I needed Dane. And Rio. *God, I needed Rio...*

I was tired and confused. So fucking confused. How was I supposed to know whether I wanted to be famous or retire from the limelight? Whether I loved Rio and wanted a life with him or accepted we were never meant to be together. Whether I wanted to live or die. Someone please tell me, because I sure as hell didn't know. I didn't know anything anymore.

To her credit, Andrea tried to engage me further, but then wasn't that what they paid her for? I was a job to her, nothing more. She didn't care about me. Why would she? She didn't even know who I was, so how could she even begin to understand the scale of my problems?

In the end though, she gave up on me, the same as everybody else did. The same taciturn orderly saw me back to my room, and then I was alone again. There were some small mercies, I suppose. Crying-woman was silent, opting now for rocking to and fro instead. I hadn't seen the shit-eater again. He was either sleeping off his hearty meal from the night before, or in hospital having his stomach pumped. Shit might not be poisonous, but I doubted eating it was good for you, even if it came out of your own arse in the first place.

I stretched out on the bed and tucked my hands behind my head. My mind replayed the events of the night before. Actually, the whole day before, from lying to KP and stealing the ticket from Dane's drawer, to turning up uninvited and confronting Rio with that lame fucking song.

*You say you can't be my happiness. You know that's not all that you are...*

Who was I trying to kid with that bullshit? Not Rio. He saw right through the song *and* me.

I was a pathetic loser. It was no wonder he'd had enough.

*Chapter Twenty-Four*

THERE WAS an electric atmosphere on the unit from the moment I woke up. I had no idea why, but when I emerged from my room for breakfast, the staff seemed to be buzzing with excitement. It was my third day being incarcerated. I'd met with Doc Andrea again the day before, but there was nothing I could say to add to what I'd already told her at our first session. She asked the same question over and over, although she attempted to phrase it differently each time. I leaned back on the couch and closed my eyes, pretending to nap. This time, it didn't take her as long to get the message and she sent me back to my room with the stern warning I wouldn't be released until I showed a willingness to engage.

The cause for the building excitement arrived shortly after lunch in the shape of one Dane Black. I don't know why I didn't see it coming. Nobody knew who the fuck I was and if they did, they didn't particularly care. But as soon as Dane showed his face, everyone creamed their panties. It drove me crazy. I wasn't jealous. Really, I wasn't. But Dane always said we were equal partners in the band when it was obvious we were far from it.

He strolled into my room like he owned the place, as at ease here as he was in his own house. I stayed sat on the side of my bed and scowled at him.

"What are you doing here?"

"The usual. Bailing out your sorry arse again."

Man, he sounded pissed. Well, boo-fucking-hoo. I didn't ask him to come. Whatever they told him, I didn't need saving. I was doing just fine and dandy, thank you very much. He should be at home with his toyboy, not running around after me.,

Fuck. Riley. If I thought Dane was mad it was nothing compared to how Riley must be feeling. I'd taken his parents' accident as an excuse to flee to another country, thinking only of myself and not caring if they were alive or dead. And now Dane left him to chase me across the Atlantic. Riley must hate my guts.

"Riley has got to be so pissed," I said.

"Oh, he's absolutely fuming," Dane answered dryly. "In fact, it wouldn't surprise me if we get back and you're not the only one who no longer has a boyfriend. His mum and dad are going to make a full recovery, by the way. Thanks for asking."

"Good, I'm glad." I saw his jaw tighten and was quick to clarify. "I mean about his parents. I'm not glad he dumped you, obviously."

"He hasn't dumped me," Dane said irritably. "Not yet anyway."

He exhaled noisily before coming to sit on the bed beside me. We'd been friends long enough for me to know when he was working himself up to saying something. It didn't take a genius to figure out I wasn't going to like it either. The only way he stood a chance of keeping Riley was if he told me to move out. It was either that or he was going to insist I went back to rehab. One, I was prepared to do for the sake of saving his relationship. The other I wasn't.

"Okay, here's how things are going to be," Dane said seriously. "The guys here are going to release you into my care. We fly home tonight, and you go straight into rehab. While you're there I'll help you find your own place for when you come out."

"No."

His eyebrows knitted together in a deep frown. "Garrison, I'm not giving you a choice in the matter."

"I don't need rehab, Dane."

"You just tried to throw yourself off the roof of the arena. You sure as hell need something."

"Okay, first of all, I wasn't drunk," I argued. "And I wasn't going to jump. I'm getting sick of saying it. If CJ had my back instead of chucking me under the bus, I wouldn't be in this shithole."

"No, you dumb shit. If it wasn't for CJ, you wouldn't be here, period. He told me what happened."

"Right, so he told you I wasn't drunk."

Dane's silence spoke volumes. Maybe CJ told Dane I was suicidal and all kinds of other bullshit, but he didn't say I was under the influence of drugs or alcohol at the time. And maybe it was time to accept I needed help of some sort, but however fucked up this situation was, it didn't require a trip to rehab. On some level Dane knew that. He just didn't see any other way of dealing with it. With me.

"I'll come home with you," I said. "I'll see a shrink and I'll move out of your house, but I'm not going to rehab. That's a deal breaker."

"What? You'd rather stay here?" Dane eyed me in bemusement.

"Here. There. What's the difference? I'm still locked up when I don't need to be. And at least here, I get to listen to Crying Woman twenty-four hours a day."

"Crying Woman?"

"Yeah, but she has nothing on Shit-eating Guy."

"Jesus, I'm not sure I even want to know." He bumped me with his shoulder, and just like that I was forgiven. "Okay, no rehab, but you get therapy."

"I will, and I'll move out," I promised. "I swear, Dane, I don't want to come between you and Riley."

"Yeah, well I swear too, Garrison. I swear if you ever do anything like this again, you better hope you succeed. Because if you don't, I'll kill you myself."

## Chapter Twenty-Five

THE FLIGHT HOME was silent for the main part. Not that we were not talking to each by choice, but both of us were exhausted, having barely slept for days for separate reasons. Even then, I didn't expect to sleep for as long as I did, but once Dane dozed off in the seat beside me, I couldn't help but do the same. It was a shame the flight wasn't longer so that I got a decent bit of shut-eye and woke up feeling refreshed. If anything, I felt worse., and if Dane's sour mood was any indication, so did he.

I bit back a sigh when the driver of the car Dane had hired pulled up outside a hotel. A classy hotel, admittedly, but not where I wanted to be. Okay, I agreed to move out of Dane's, but I didn't realise I was barred from the premises without even being allowed to get any of my stuff.

"I'll have someone bring over a change of clothes later," Dane said, having the decency to look a little shamefaced. He knew what he was doing was a shit move.

"Tell Riley I'm sorry."

"If he's talking to me I will." He gave me a grim smile as I climbed out of the car. "I meant what I said before, Garrison. This is absolutely the last time I'm going to save you from yourself. You mess up again, and you're on your own."

I nodded, not knowing what there was to say to make him feel any better, He didn't believe I could keep my nose clean. He was just waiting for me to fail. To fuck my life up again and let him down. At least, when I did, I wouldn't be betraying his trust. How could I when he didn't have any trust in me to begin with?

And I would fail, because that was what I did. Failing was the only thing I was good at. Well, that and playing guitar, but where did that get me? Fame and fortune, sure, but I could be the greatest guitarist in the world, and I still wouldn't be happy. If I was honest, I didn't blame Dane. I had no more faith in me staying out of trouble than he did.

He spared me the embarrassment of escorting me to my room, although the car waited at the kerb until I entered the lavish foyer. I wrinkled my nose in distaste as I crossed the marbled floor. A place like this would never have been my first choice. It was expensive, but I could afford it. That wasn't the issue. I didn't need to be surrounded by luxury, even in the short term. Something a little more basic would have suited me just fine, but God forbid Garrison Swann let the side down by staying anywhere less than fabulous.

My room turned out to be more of a suite and I groaned inwardly. Anyone would think I was here for the duration. I didn't need all this. All I needed was a shower and a bed. That was enough for any man. Oh, and somewhere to recharge my phone. You know... just in case Rio called to make sure I was still alive.

I showered quickly and dried off before wrapping myself in a plush white bathrobe. Then I stretched out on the bed and made myself comfortable. Sleep eluded me though. Despite being tired and not having slept for long enough on the plane, my eyes wouldn't stay shut. I was restless. On edge. The urge to do something irresponsible built up inside me until I couldn't ignore it anymore, however hard I tried.

Fuck, I hadn't even been left to my own devices for an hour yet, and already I was on the verge of doing something crazy. Guess I really wasn't to be trusted. I couldn't help myself though. I had to move. Get out of this room and go somewhere. Anywhere...

Okay, now I was lying to myself as well as everyone else. There was no *anywhere* about it. I knew exactly where I was going. The only question was how I was going to get there, and even then, a plan was slowly forming in my mind. It was a crazy one. Like mega crazy. And inarguably illegal, but what harm did it do to break a few laws here and there? Dane would be furious, and Rio would be as pissed as hell, but I was past caring.

I dressed again and grabbed my phone, wallet and keys. Funny how nobody had thought to question why I had door keys when I had no house to match them. Knowing how everyone liked to spy on me and run to Dane telling tales, I took the stairs to the ground floor and slipped out through the service entrance at the back of the hotel. A short bus ride later and I stood on the pavement outside Rio's townhouse.

Oh, he was going to lose his shit when he found out what I was up to.

I let myself in the front door and disabled the alarm. Technically, I wasn't breaking and entering. If Rio didn't want me to have a set of keys, he shouldn't have left his lying about so I could take them and get copies. Just like he shouldn't have let me see him enter the code to disarm the alarm. He was practically begging me to do exactly what I just had.

Going through to the kitchen I opened the key safe on the wall. For all his security-consciousness, Rio was making it way too easy for me. The hooks were even labelled with which lock each key was for. I helped myself to the two keys that I had come here for, and just as I closed the door, my phone rang.

I smirked, seeing Rio's name flash up on the screen. I didn't doubt that he would have received some sort of alert as soon as I entered the house, but he'd called quicker than expected.

"Hey," I answered casually. "I thought you blocked me."

"I did," he snapped, "but then I had to unblock you because, yet again, you broke into my house."

"I didn't break in. I've got keys."

"For fuck's sake, Garrison..." He took a deep breath, trying to calm himself. "Why are you there? What are you doing?"

"Nothing bad, I promise. I'm just borrowing a couple of things."

He paused. "Like what?"

"Stuff," I said evasively.

"Garrison..." His tone was threatening, although I don't know what he thought he could do to stop me when he was over three thousand miles away.

"Rio," I countered. "Don't worry about it. You just go on with your tour and forget about me."

Rio snorted. "Yeah, I tried that. Didn't work out so well, when you turn up here suicidal and then break into my house and steal shit from me."

"Uh, I wasn't suicidal and I'm *borrowing* shit, not stealing it," I corrected. "It's only a couple of keys. No biggie."

"Keys to what exactly?"

Was that a note of worry in his voice?

"You know..." I shrugged, even though he couldn't see me. Or maybe he could. It wouldn't surprise me if he had cameras all over the place, same as at the cottage. "Keys to the place where you tried to drown me."

It was his fault I'd fallen into the river, after all.

"The Corvette."

I heard him inhale sharply. Right, he cared about somethings then, just not me.

"You'd better not even think about touching my fucking car."

"Relax. You'll get it back in one piece." Probably.

"You can't even drive!"

"I know, but how hard can it be? I've seen other people do it."

"Garrison..."

"Got to go, babe. I've got a long drive ahead of me."

"Don't hang up on me!"

"Love you, Bye."

I smiled childishly as I switched off my phone and tucked it into my pocket. Time to get moving. If Rio called the police, I'd be arrested before I even got the Corvette out of the garage. Or maybe he'd have them meet me at the cottage, assuming I didn't crash and die on route. Worse still, maybe he'd call Dane and finally reveal his big secret, telling him where to find the cottage *and* me. Then again, Dane swore I was on my final last chance and would be disowned the next time I did anything stupid. Stealing a car I couldn't possibly hope to drive would be considered stupid in anybody's book, so if Dane was true to his word, he'd hang up on Rio anyway, and tell him he didn't want to know.

My heart was in my throat as I entered the private parking garage where Rio kept his Corvette. The car was a beast, a monster created from gleaming red metal and chrome. As first cars went, it probably wasn't the best option, but if the car was making a statement, then so was I. Sliding behind the wheel, I adjusted the seat so that I could reach the pedals, surprised at how much longer Rio's legs had to be compared to my own.

With trembling fingers, I put the key in the ignition and started the engine. The car practically purred like a cat. I'd never been a car person but, in this instance, I could see the attraction. I put my hands on the wheel, positioning them at ten to two like the hands of a clock, because I seemed to remember reading that somewhere. Cautiously, I pressed on the accelerator, and the engine roared.

Fuck, if anyone was going to come charging in and stop me, they really needed to get here like *now*!

The car crept slowly forward. Holy shit, I was driving! I could do this. At a snail's pace maybe, but I was doing it. It was a minor miracle that I wasn't stopped by the police for driving so unhurriedly through the city streets, but once I got onto the motorway I began to relax slightly and put my foot down. I stuck to the slow lane though and let everyone fly past me in the other lanes. I didn't care. It probably made their day to overtake a Corvette, and – contrary to popular belief – I didn't want to die.

I'd much rather both me and the car arrived at the cottage in one piece.

# Chapter Twenty-Six

AT LEAST I didn't have to break in this time. I just let myself in the back door with Rio's key and waved at the empty kitchen, knowing Rio was probably watching me on his damn concealed cameras. Despite my death-defying jaunt along the motorway and narrow, winding Devon roads, I felt a weight lift from my shoulders as I closed the kitchen door behind me. Oh, I was still in a world of trouble, I didn't doubt that, but this place felt like coming home. More so than Dane's, and Rio's town-house, or even any place of my own. Would Rio sell it to me, I wondered, because I realised I didn't just want any old cottage by the sea. I wanted this one.

I opened the fridge and helped myself to a bottle of water. Boring, I know, but I was determined not to drink myself into oblivion for once. The police could turn up at any moment and arrest me, or Dane could arrive and be angry enough to beat me to death, but that wasn't the reason I wanted to stay alert and clear headed. Whatever time I was graced with at the cottage, I wanted to enjoy. Remember it. I hoped I would have the chance to sit by the river and watch the boats go by, which was peaceful and calming. I'd do my best not to fall in this time.

Also, I was sure Rio would be watching and I wanted to prove to him I could stay sober when left to my own devices. I helped myself to something to eat from the freezer, and even washed up and put the plate and cutlery away when I'd finished. *See, Rio, I can be domesticated.* Then I grabbed another bottle of water and carried it upstairs to the bedroom.

Without the onrush of adrenaline to keep me going, jet-lag was kicking my arse. I needed to sleep.

"Do you have cameras in here too?" I mused out loud, as I stripped down to my t-shirt and shorts and slipped beneath the duvet. "Do you save the recordings of us fucking like rabbits and watch them over and over again?"

I smiled at the idea he had us on film. Those were some videos I wouldn't mind watching myself. I'd never asked him if he had a hidden camera in the bedroom, but it wouldn't surprise me. He had them all over the rest of the house. Just because I hadn't found them yet, didn't mean they weren't there.

"I wish I had my guitar," I said with a yawn. "I could finish your song."

I reached for the bedside lamp. "I love you, Rio. Whether you love me back or not, it doesn't change how I feel about you."

## Chapter Twenty-Seven

I SLEPT FOR HOURS. When I finally opened my eyes and they stayed open for longer than five seconds, the sun was high in the sky. The need to piss was borderline urgent, and I was starving. Still bleary eyed, and with a fuzzy head, I rolled out of bed and staggered to the bathroom. Feeling markedly better once I'd relieved myself; I made my way down the stairs. Just as I entered the kitchen, I heard someone knocking on the door, and my heart sank. Stupidly, I thought I'd have more time at the cottage before being busted by either the police or Dane.

Surprisingly, I found neither when I answered the door, but was faced instead with a middle-aged delivery man holding a large package. I took it from him, signed his electronic pad with the tip of my finger and closed the door. I carried the parcel through to the kitchen and set it down on the table. What the hell? It was addressed to me, but nobody knew I was here. Or if they did, they didn't know where *here* was. Except for Rio, obviously, but he was hardly likely to send me anything.

I took a knife from the drawer and carefully sliced open the large box. Then I hesitated, afraid to unfold the cardboard flaps. What if there was something horrible inside? Some sort of death threat? Rio might not send me anything like that, but Cage would. Only, that was stupid, because Cage didn't know where the cottage was any more than Dane. And the box was quite large and heavy. What kind of death threat was heavy? I mean, I was no expert, but didn't they usually come on pieces of paper with letters cut from magazines? Unless that was just on the telly.

*For fuck's sake, man up, Garrison.* I flipped open the box and stopped, staring at the contents in bewilderment. It was a guitar. A beautifully crafted, dark wood acoustic guitar. Jesus, did Rio hear me last night when I said I wished I had my guitar? He'd never mentioned sound being a part of his security system, but it was either that or he was a fucking amazing lip-reader.

I lifted the guitar from the box with the reverence it deserved. Underneath it was a small card. Opening it, I read one word. *Yes.* Not Rio's handwriting obviously, but I didn't doubt the gift was from him. He'd obviously told them what to put in the card, but what did he mean? Yes, finish the song? It had to be. Even if he was able to hear me or had lip-reading as a hidden talent. I hadn't asked him a direct question. Unless...

Shit. I had, hadn't I? I asked him if he watched the recordings of us having sex. Was this him admitting that he did? Because that was kind of hot. What's more, if he was replaying scenes of us fucking and sending me wildly expensive gifts, it meant he wasn't as done with me as he claimed. We weren't over and there was still a chance he would forgive me.

I stepped into the middle of the room; the guitar cradled in my arms.

"Thank you," I said out loud, not knowing if he was watching me on live stream or if he would play it back later. "I'll finish your song, Rio, but using the cameras is cheating. If you want the rest of it, baby, you can damn well come and get it."

With that, I carried my new guitar outside, heading for the river. Rio would have a shit-fit when he realised my destination, probably imagining I would throw myself in at the first opportunity. I had no intention of going into the water, though. Not with my new baby in my arms. The guitar could sound like shit, but I'd still treasure it because it wasn't just a gift from Rio. It was hope wrapped up in wood and steel alloy strings.

Even so, I carefully picked my way down the short wooden jetty and sat on the end, dangling my feet over the water. I took my time tuning the guitar, please and surprised at the sweet tone it produced. Of course, I should have known Rio wouldn't buy me any old rubbish. What he'd sent me was a quality instrument. I only hoped I could do it justice.

For the next few hours, I sat by the gently flowing river and played, pausing only to wave to the occasional boat as it passed by. I ran through a few Jaded Intent tracks and made progress on Rio's song. Eventually, though, I had to admit my fingers were numb and I was frozen to the bone. Not taking any chances, I shuffled away from the edge before clambering to my feet.

"Hi, honey, I'm home," I called out as I walked into the house.

There was no answer, but I didn't expect one. Maybe I was losing the plot, talking to Rio like he was in the house and not on a tour bus or in a hotel on the other side of the Atlantic. Our relationship had taken its fair share of twists and turns over the years, but this had to be the strangest yet. On the other hand, it was undoubtedly the best we'd ever gotten along. Or – at least – the longest we'd gone without arguing.

Days passed. I felt guilty at times, for not contacting Dane, but overall, I was content. I slept a lot. Sat by the river and played my sweet, new guitar. Ate regular meals and abstained from the booze. I even started reading a book I found in the living room. Some thriller about gay vampires, which I wouldn't have thought was Rio would be into at all, but here it was in his house. I was beginning to feel like a whole new person.

But at the same time, I was waiting. I knew Rio was on tour in America, with shows almost every night, but I truly believed that – sooner or later – he would come.

Sometime during the fifth night since I'd been staying at the cottage, I was woken by a heavy weight across my back. I cracked open my eyes, although it was too dark to see the end of my nose, let alone beyond it. There was a figure in the bed with me.

Not that I was worried. I'd recognise the weight of his arm anywhere. The sound of his soft breathing. The scent of his shampoo...

Rio was home. And he wasn't shouting and screaming or manhandling me out of his house as he was probably entitled to do. Instead, he quietly crawled into bed and put his arm around me. I mean, jetlag was a bitch for sure, but even if he was too tired to get into a fight from the off, he wouldn't want to cuddle if he was angry. There was only one message a warm embrace was going to send, and it wasn't *I hate you. Get the fuck out of my house.*

"Does this mean I'm forgiven?"

"No," Rio grumbled sleepily. "It means I'm too knackered right now to kick the shit out of you."

I shuffled closer and kissed him lightly. I was aiming for his mouth, but I couldn't see in the dark and planted a smacker on the end of his nose instead. Rio made a small sound of pleasure and I smiled. Even though it was an accident, it was the first time I'd done anything soppy and sentimental, like kiss him any place other than on the lips. Rio seemed to like it, although I had to wonder if he would let me if he wasn't half asleep.

"I hope you're not trying to start anything," he mumbled.

"Nope, just saying hello."

"Mmmm."

"I love you."

This time, my answer was a soft snore. Rio was out for the count. Jet-lag aside, who knew when he last slept? I didn't imagine he got much on tour, with Cage and Mal wanting to party every minute they weren't on stage. And his flight wouldn't have been long enough to get any decent shut-eye on the plane. Added to all the stress I'd put him through recently, and it was no wonder he was exhausted.

It was no surprise either, when I was the first to wake up a few hours later. I eased out from beneath Rio's arm and got out of bed, turning to tug the duvet over Rio's shoulders. He muttered in his sleep, before snuggling down under the cover.

Leaving him to his much-needed slumber, I dressed quickly and went downstairs to use the toilet so I could flush without disturbing him.

I made myself a coffee and carried both it and my phone outside. There was a painted bench at the front of the house which faced the river, so that was where I sat. The last thing I wanted was for Rio to wake up, look out of the window and see me perched on the end of the pier. He'd have a heart attack.

There was still a chill in the air, despite the sun shining brightly overhead. Spring was trying to muscle its way in, but the last vestiges of winter clung on with determination. I sat sideways on the bench and hugged my knees to my chest for warmth.

For the first time since fleeing London, I switched on my phone. Instantly, I was bombarded with a long list of notifications. Messages flooded my inbox. Dane outnumbered everyone else by far, which was to be expected. The rest were from KP, Nelson and Dozer, and Mike, our manager. Only one from Rio, but then he'd have known not to bother because I would turn my phone off for the exact reason of making sure nobody could get hold of me. I'd have been more offended if he kept trying, because that would prove he didn't know me at all. Which didn't say much for Dane after decades of friendship, but he was different. I was glad he'd kept trying because it meant he hadn't given up on me yet like he said he was going to.

I opened several messages with no name attached, just a number. They were all from Cage, whose colourful choice of language spelled out exactly what he was going to do to me when he got hold of me. I was pretty sure a lot of what he'd written constituted death threats, but that was Cage for you. He'd always been somewhat volatile.

The real shocker was the sight of Riley's name on the list. Why the hell would Riley message me, not once but three times? Riley hated me. He ought to be glad I'd run off again.

When I came out here with my phone, I had every intention of calling Dane to let him know I was alive, and he could stop worrying. Now though, curiosity got the better of me. It could be a trick; Dane messaging from Riley's phone when I wouldn't answer him, but it didn't make sense. He had to know I was even less likely to respond to Riley.

Unless it piqued my curiosity...

Which it had...

But what did it matter anyway? I had to speak to Dane at some point, so it was no biggie if I called Riley's phone and it was Dane who answered.

I hit the call button before I could change my mind.

"About fucking time," Riley spat in lieu of a more formal greeting. "Where the hell are you?"

"I'm with Rio, so tell Dane he can relax."

"I said *where*, not who."

"I heard what you said, but I'm *with* Rio, so I can't tell you *where*. As far as I know, this place is still a secret."

"Yeah, well, wherever you are, do me a favour and don't come back," Riley said coldly. "Give Dane a fair shot at finally getting over you."

Ouch. I guess I deserved that. I knew Dane got his panties in a twist every time I pulled a disappearing act, but I never really stopped to consider how deeply it affected him, not knowing if I was safe, or dead in a ditch somewhere.

"I'm sorry," I said, meaning it for quite possibly the first time in my life. Or maybe the second, because the song I'd written for Rio was an apology of sorts and I meant every word.

"You should be." Some of the anger drained from his voice, so those two little words must have sounded convincing to his ears. "You've got to stop doing this, Garrison. And, if you can't stop, you need to make a clean break. Let Dane build a life without you in it."

"I thought he already was. With you."

Riley snorted. "So did I, but he chooses you over me time after time. I think he always will, and I can't live like that."

"You're wrong. Dane loves you. He worships the ground you work on."

Another snort. "He has a funny way of showing it a lot of the time."

"I know, and I'll stay away if that's what you want." It would be like cutting off a limb, but I'd do it if I had to. I owed Dane that much. "He's ready to give up on me, okay? He told me himself, he chooses you over me."

"Then why hasn't he?" Riley asked sulkily. "Why is he still chasing after you?"

"I don't know. Maybe because he feels responsible for me being the way I am."

Oops. I hadn't meant for it to come out like that. I'd never told a soul about Dane's involvement, not even Rio. It was not something Dane and I ever discussed, but both of us knew the guilt and shame he'd felt over the years. He wasn't to blame for my addictive personality, but he hadn't helped either in the beginning. We'd been young and stupid. Dane couldn't have foreseen the trouble caused by one immature action.

"Why would Dane feel responsible for the way you are, Garrison?" Riley's voice was dangerously low.

He didn't believe me. He thought I was making excuses, laying my shit firmly at Dane's door, and letting him take the rap for my being such a horrible person. In the long run, it was for the best if Riley saw me as the bad guy. Rather than Dane, who'd spent his whole adult life trying to atone for a mistake he made when he was little more than a kid.

"It's nothing forget it."

"No, I can't forget it. You've said it now. What is it Dane supposedly did to turn you into a drug-addicted, alcoholic arsehole?"

"You know, just for that, I'm going to tell you," I snapped, because I got it, I really did, but I was sick of his shitty attitude towards me. "It's not his fault I'm an addict, that's on me. But guess who gave me my first line of coke? Dane scored it. Dane brought it to my apartment. We got high together every night for two weeks, and then Dane decided he didn't like it and he stopped. Only... surprise, surprise... I couldn't stop. I was already hooked."

"You're lying. Dane has never touched drugs."

"Not since then he hasn't. And, in all honesty, I probably would have gone down the booze and drugs road anyway. It's hard to avoid in my line of work. But I'll never know for sure, because Dane started me off before we were even famous."

"I don't believe you." Riley's voice, so strident and aggressive a few short minutes ago, was now barely above a whisper. Contrary to his words, he knew I was telling him the truth.

"Believe what you want. You asked me a question and I answered it." I sighed, feeling the conversation had veered off track somehow. I was trying to persuade Riley to stay with Dane, not put him off the guy altogether. "Listen, Riley, all my problems are of my own making. Dane blames himself, but I don't. I never have. All that shit happened a long time ago. We were kids."

"I understand that, but..."

"But nothing. Dane needs to get over it, and so do you. He loves you. Don't give up on him because of something he did years before he met you."

"Fine," Riley said sourly. "But I need to tell him I know. You should be there too. It's your forgiveness he's searching for."

"I thought you wanted me to stay away?"

"I do, but this is for Dane's sake." Riley was suddenly firm in tone again now that he was defending his man. "He needs to apologise, and he needs to hear you say you accept it."

"Whatever way you want to play it," I agreed. "But you need to know something too. There's never been anything I felt I should forgive him for. Dane's the one who can't forgive himself."

# Chapter Twenty-Eight

"UGH! THAT'S COLD."

I smiled in amusement at the disgust on Rio's face. He'd plonked down on the bench beside me and stolen a swig of my long since forgotten coffee before I could warn him it had sat there for hours untouched.

"Serves you right," I reprimanded teasingly. "You shouldn't take what isn't yours."

Rio gave me an incredulous look. He still had dark circles of exhaustion under his eyes, but he'd showered and shaved and seemed to have put the worst of his jet-lag behind him.

"Are you serious, right now?"

"How do you mean?" I asked innocently.

"What the fuck do you think I mean? You broke into *two* of my houses. Stole my car. You've been eating my food. Shit, the coffee came out of my cupboard, so it's mine to begin with!" The sparkle in his eyes belied his words. He was only pretending to be mad. "Kind of the pot calling the kettle black, don't you think?"

"Maybe." I shrugged. "I guess it's a good job you love me."

"Who told you that?" Rio scoffed, poking me in the ribs with his finger.

I squirmed away from him with an unmanly giggle.

"Uh, you did. When you sent me the guitar. When you left your tour to come back here... which Cage is literally going to murder me for, by the way. When you admitted to watching the tapes of you fucking the shit out of me."

Rio arched an eyebrow. "When did I admit to that?"

"On the post-it note. You said 'yes'. Isn't that what you were referring to?"

He smirked. "Maybe. What are you doing out here anyway? It's warmer inside."

"Yeah, I know." Although I wasn't really feeling the cold at that point. Either I'd become accustomed to the chill in the air, or the temperature had risen a few degrees and Rio didn't notice it because he'd just left a nice warm bed. "I've been sat here thinking."

"About?"

"Oh, you know. Everything. Life, love and the universe. And guinea-pigs."

Rio's lips quirked in a combination of curiosity and amusement.

"And what, pray tell, is your considered opinion?"

"On what?"

"All of it. Any of it." He paused. "But specifically... the guinea-pigs."

I grinned at him. "I like them. I think I might get a couple and call them Dane and Cage."

"I think you've pissed Cage off enough for one lifetime, without adding insult to injury." he reclined on the bench, resting one arm along the backrest so he could stroke the back of my neck with his fingertips. "Where are you going to keep these guinea-pigs? Last I heard, you're basically homeless."

"Ah, well..." I hesitated, hoping he wouldn't take what I was about to say the wrong way. "I was hoping you'd sell me this place."

Rio's eyes widened in surprise. "You want to buy the cottage?"

I tried to make him understand. This wasn't greed or playing games. I wasn't trying to fuck with his head or his heart. This place meant the world to me.

"I'm different when I'm here," I explained, staring out across the grass to the river. I was a coward, afraid to meet his eyes in case he gave me an outright no. If I couldn't persuade him, I'd probably cry. Then he'd accuse me of faking my tears to guilt trip him into giving me what I wanted. "I'm happier. Calmer. More relaxed. My head's clear when I'm here, and I feel closer to you, even when you're not around. I thought I wanted a house by the sea, but it's more than that. I want *this* house."

Rio regarded me silently. Even though I stared straight ahead, I could feel the intensity of his gaze on my face. His fingers stilled against my skin, although he didn't break contact.

"I'm not selling you my house, Garrison," he said eventually, and I was embarrassed by the speed at which my eyes overflowed with tears. Why was I so hurt when I'd expected him to refuse all along? "But I'll give it to you."

"Wait... what?"

I turned my head to gape at him, certain I must have misheard. He was giving me an hour to get the hell out of his house and his life was probably nearer to what he'd actually said.

But Rio was smiling, which confused the shit out of me. He raised his free hand and gently brushed the tears from my cheeks with his thumb.

"I'll sign it over to you, exactly as it is, on one proviso. When I'm not working away, I get to stay here with you."

Was he serious? I searched his face for the lie, but all I saw staring back at me was honesty. And love.

Jesus Christ, after everything I put him through. How could he still love me?

"Why would you want to?" I whispered, in total awe of this beautiful man. "How can you trust me after..."

Okay, I needed to shut the fuck up before I talked him into changing his mind.

"We still have some work to do on the trust thing," Rio said lightly. "And you can pay me for the house by playing the rest of the song, if you like."

"Sooo,,, you're not going to kick my arse for stealing your car?"

"I'll *fuck* your arse later, but for now, I want to hear my song."

"You're really giving me your house in exchange for a shitty song?"

"I said so, didn't I?" Rio rolled his eyes impatiently. "Just play the damn song."

"Oh my God!" I squealed dramatically, pressing a hand to my chest. "Some people are *so* needy."

Rio smirked. "Tell me about it. There's this guy I know, made me come all the way home from America to listen to an apparently shitty song he wrote, even though I'm supposed to be on tour with my band."

"Wow! Sounds like a real douchebag," I breathed, looking at Rio like I was innocence personified. "You should dump him."

"Believe me, I've tried." Rio narrowed his eyes, his attempt to appear menacing failing miserably in the light of his broad smile. "He's not that easy to get rid of."

"Is that so? Why not?"

I crawled onto his lap and straddled his impressively firm thighs. Rio's hands went to my hips and pulled me closer.

"Well, he's kind of clingy for a start."

"Hmm, sounds desperate if you ask me."

"Oh, he's definitely desperate." Another tug on my hips. We were chest to chest now. Nose to nose. I could feel his breath on my lips as, further South, his dick hardened against mine. "But what can I do? I'm desperate too. Desperately in love with him."

"Maybe you should try telling him once in a while."

Again with the shut-your-mouth-Garrison. Don't spoil the moment by acting like a prick.

"Maybe you should sing me my song so I can take you upstairs and fuck your brains out after."

"Can't we fuck before?"

"Nope."

Rio shot his arms out without warning and shoved me from his lap. With a yelp, I flew backwards and landed on the grass. I glared up at Rio, but his laughter was infectious, and I couldn't keep myself from smiling.

"Fine," I grumbled as I picked myself up off the ground. "But just so you know, my dick is so hard I could play the guitar with it, and it wouldn't even hurt if it got caught in the strings."

"Now that I'd like to see," Rio said, eyes alight with enthusiasm. "Quick. Get your guitar before you go soft."

"You're an idiot." I scowled at him over my shoulder as I headed for the front door.

"I know you are, but what am I?"

God, we were so childish.

# Chapter Twenty-Nine

SOMEHOW, we ended up in the bedroom anyway. I sat with my back to the headboard, guitar in lap, while Rio perched, facing me, at the end of the bed.

Somehow, we also ended up wearing nothing but out underpants. We both knew where this was going. Me. Him. Naked and sweating. Making up and reconnecting in a way only we could. It would be hard and fast, and that was perfectly fine with me.

But... song first. Sex after.

"Just remember," I said, running my fingers over the strings. "I'm a musician, not a vocalist."

"Think yourself lucky." Rio snorted. "I'm a drummer, so I'm not even a musician in most people's eyes." He lowered his gaze with a frown. "Including yours apparently."

"You know I didn't mean that." He was referring to all the verbal shit I'd thrown his way when I lost it at Carnival's pre-tour bash. That was almost a month ago, yet it was still playing on his mind. Maybe I wasn't as forgiven as I thought I was. "I was high and drunk and insanely jealous. I didn't know what I was saying."

"You should have trusted me." Rio lifted troubled eyes to meet mine. "Wasn't it clear I wanted to be exclusive when I asked you to move in with me?"

"Uh, not really. The only thing you made clear was that it was a temporary arrangement and then you were leaving to go on tour."

Rio seemed a little taken aback by my words, as if I was describing a scene he didn't recognise. How could he perceive his actions so differently to me? One of us had read the situation entirely wrong, and I was damn sure it wasn't me.

The air between us was suddenly charged with the wrong kind of tension. Sexual tension, I was all for, but this was another kind. This was the sort of tension that led to a full-blown argument, and I didn't want to fight. why did being together have to be so fucking hard the whole time?

"Can we just drop it?" I pleaded. "I'm sorry, okay. Sorry for every shitty thing I've ever said or done to you. I'm a mess, Rio, and I probably always will be. The night of the party, I was so hurt and angry. I thought I was losing you, and when Mal said–"

"Mal?" Rio interrupted sharply. He was immediately furious, and not with me for a change. "Let me guess, he told you I was going to cheat on you. Or that I already had. Then he loaded you up with Oxy and sent you back to the party to cause havoc."

"Something like that," I muttered. "But he didn't put a drink in my hand, and he didn't force me to punch you."

"No, he just wound you up like a clockwork toy and let you go." Rio shook his head, irritated at himself for only having it figured it out so late in the game. "I promise you, Garrison, this is the last time I will ever work with that ratbag-bastard. If he doesn't quit Carnival, then I will."

"What? No, you can't do that. Not because of me."

"I'm doing it *for* you," Rio argued. "What Mal did put you on that rooftop in New York. You could have been killed."

"But I wasn't. I'm right here. *We're* here." I stuck my leg out and nudged him with my foot. "So, can I play this stupid song now or what?"

Rio waved a hand as if to say go ahead, but it was plain to see he was still fuming over what Mal had done. Knowing my luck, he wouldn't even listen properly, and as soon as I was done with the song, we'd go right back to arguing over events that had already happened and things we couldn't hope to change.

But as soon as I began to play Rio's shoulders relaxed and he focused all his attention on my fingers as they danced over the strings. I had him hooked, whatever other people said, even in jest, Rio was a musician. He responded to the music with his heart and soul, just the same way I did.

I began to sing. Softly at first, then more loudly as my confidence grew.

*YOU SAY YOU CAN'T BE MY HAPPINESS*
    *You know it's not all that you are*
    *You are the air that I breathe*
    *My life. My soul. My heart*

*YOU ARE MY REASON FOR LIVING*
    *You are the reason I wake*
    *You are the guiding light in my darkness*
    *You are every good decision I make*

*YOU SAY YOU CAN'T BE MY HAPPINESS*
    *But without you I'm not happy at all*
    *Because you are the only one I can love*
    *The one who catches me whenever I fall*

*YOU SAY YOU CAN'T BE MY HAPPINESS*
    *You know it's not all that you are*
    *You are the air that I breathe*
    *My life. My soul. My heart*

. . .

*YOU SAY YOU CAN'T BE MY HAPPINESS*
  *But, baby, there's no man I want more*
  *No man who owns me like you do*
  *Yours is the love I've been waiting for*


*YOU SAY YOU CAN'T BE MY HAPPINESS*
  *But that's what I need you to be*
  *I need you to stand right here by my side*
  *Because without you, there is no me*


*YOU SAY YOU CAN'T BE MY HAPPINESS*
  *You know it's not all that you are*
  *You are the air that I breathe*
  *My life. My soul. My heart*


THE LAST CHORD FADED INTO SILENCE; RIO DIDN'T SPEAK. He continued to sit and stare at the guitar in my lap, his expression unreadable. My heart clenched and I felt sick to the stomach with disappointment. He hated it.

"Sorry," I mumbled, sniffing back tears. For fuck's sake, I wasn't going to cry in front of Rio again. He'd see it as emotional blackmail. "There's no pressure, okay. it's just a stu–"

Rio lunged. I yelped as he yanked on my ankles and pulled me halfway down the bed. He landed on top of me, and my first thought was for the guitar sandwiched between our bodies. But then he kissed me, and the guitar was forgotten, along with everything else that had nothing to do with the feel of Rio's lips on mine. Or his tongue delving into my mouth. Or his hands, roughly caressing every part of my body they could reach.

Which obviously wasn't enough to satisfy Rio, because he growled in frustration and reared up before shoving the guitar onto the floor. Oh, well... he paid for it. I guess he had the right to break it, if he felt like it. I might care later, but right now my dick didn't give a toss. It was too busy doing its own little happy dance as Rio peeled my underwear down my legs.

He grabbed the lube from the bedside drawer and wasted no time in spreading me open. Even so, I was squirming with impatience by the time he withdrew his fingers and replaced them with the tip of his cock.

"Are you ready for this?"

"You know I am."

I was already panting like a dog, pre-cum dripping from my dick like a leaking tap. Whatever he had to give, I would take. I was a greedy bitch when it came to fucking Rio. I wanted it all.

He slammed into me. My back arched from the bed, and I cried out in pain and pleasure combined. The burn soon faded as Rio snapped his hips, driving into me with all the finesse of a jackhammer.

This was us. It was what Dane and Cage would never be able to understand. They called it hate-sex, but to us it was making love. Whether we were angry, making up, saying hello or goodbye, or just plain horny – the sex was no different. Hot, raw and violent. *This* was the sex we enjoyed.

Rio pulled out, leaving me whimpering at the sudden, yawning emptiness. He flipped me onto my stomach and filled me again with fast, punishing thrusts.

Fuck, I was going to come without even touching myself the way Rio was hammering my arse. Then again, it was a case of having to, because Rio had my hands tightly gripped above my head. He was going to leave bruises, but who cared? Not me.

I pressed my dick into the mattress, groaning at the sweet friction that came each time Rio's weight shunted me forward. From his ragged breathing, I could tell that Rio was close too.

Moments later, his rhythm faltered. Rio's teeth clamped down my shoulder, the sharp sting enough to trigger my own blinding orgasm. Rio collapsed on top of me, neither of us possessing the energy required to move.

"Fuck me, Rio," I breathed, when I was capable of coherent speech again.

"Thought I just did."

"Oh, you absolutely did," I chuckled. "I'll be feeling you for days; my shoulder as much as my arse."

"Good, at least you won't forget who you belong to."

"That's not fair, Rio. I never know if you mean it when you say shit like that."

"I mean it." He kissed the bite mark on my shoulder. "I know we've still got a lot to figure out if we're going to make this work, but I want to try. I love you. I'm not ready to give up on us yet."

He slipped his softening dick from my hole, before delivering a resounding slap to my backside.

"Ow! What was that for?"

"Don't call my song stupid." he scowled at me in mock seriousness.

I smiled back at him. "You like it then?"

"I more than like it. Have you given it a title?"

"Not really." I folded my arms under my head and yawned, ready for a post-orgasm nap. "I've just been calling it the song for Rio."

"Song for Rio," the man himself repeated with a radiant smile. "It's perfect."

<h1 style="text-align:center">Chapter Thirty</h1>

THE NEXT DAY, Rio invited Dane and Riley to the cottage. I was probably more shocked than they were. Rio had kept the location of the cottage secret for so many years. I hated the idea he was being forced into revealing its whereabouts because of me.

As usual, Rio had a different viewpoint. The cottage wasn't his to hide anymore. By the end of the week, it would be mine. And whereas for him it had been a part-time bolthole, for me the cottage would be a permanent home. People needed to know where I was, especially Dane. It would be even more important when Rio was away.

Personally, I would rather have spent a few more days in seclusion with Rio before we began socialising with other people again. Other people and their opinions were usually the point at which our relationship went tits-up. Contained in our little bubble, our relationship was strong, and we were very much in love. As soon as our friends and bandmates interfered, we could barely speak to each other without descending into an argument.

Grudgingly, I had to admit Rio right in this instance. My track record proved I didn't function well on my own. Even though Rio swore blind he loved me and wanted to be with me, there were no guarantees I wouldn't slip back into a deep depression when he went back to

Carnival. Someone needed to know where I was, so they keep an eye on me. And for all my promises to give him and Riley space, that someone had to be Dane. I didn't have anyone else I could trust, and Dane wouldn't stand for being replaced anyway.

Om the plus side to their visit, Dane had retrieved my bag from the hotel and was bringing me some clean clothes to wear. Not that I was wearing much in the way of clothing when Rio was around. Dane and Riley were not due until mid-afternoon, so Rio insisted on spending the morning in bed, giving me a few more marks of ownership. He hadn't said when he was leaving yet, but it was bound to be sooner rather than later.

By the time Riley's modest, little car pulled up alongside Rio's red Corvette, my legs were like jelly, and I could hardly move. Rio certainly had plenty of new material to add to his wank-bank.

Rio ordered food and the four of us squeezed around the small kitchen table to eat. Dane and Rio didn't take much persuading to stuff their faces, and even I tucked in, having worked up an appetite with the morning's vigorous workout. Only Riley seemed to be holding back. Several times, I noticed the way his gaze flicked between me and Dane. Please God, don't let him be building up to another jealous rant. I thought we were over that. Riley was the one who insisted on this meeting, even though I'd offered to stay away. Dane didn't seem to notice anything amiss, so Riley obviously hadn't mentioned what he knew just yet.

"So, are you guys back together?" I asked. "Properly, I mean. Clearly, you're together right now."

"We're taking it slowly," Dane replied, reaching over to squeeze Riley's hand. "Riley hasn't moved back in yet, but we see each other almost every day. We're going on dates this time, instead of diving in with both feet like before."

"Good, I'm glad." I made sure I was looking at Riley when I smiled and said, "I'm sorry I messed it up for you."

Dane shrugged. "In a way, you did us a favour." he looked at Riley fondly. "We know we love each other, so there's no rush. We want this to be forever. Not burn out after a few months like…" he cleared his throat awkwardly. "So... um... what about you two? Have you kissed and made up?"

"More than kissed," Riley pointed out, his cheeks turning a cute shade of pink. "Garrison looks like Rio tried to eat him."

I touched my fingers to the bruises on my neck and laughed.

"These are just the ones you can see." I leaned across the table in a conspiratorial whisper. "He swallows too."

"Jesus, Garrison, give it a rest, will you." Rio lightly punched my shoulder, but he wasn't really annoyed. If anything, he was amused. "In answer to your question, Dane, we're in the same situation as you and Riley. We've got shit to work on, I'm not denying that. But we love each other. We want to be together and we're both prepared to change, if that's what it takes to make *us* happen."

Dane nodded like he understood, but his expression said he was sceptical. I had a feeling he doubted my ability to adapt more than he doubted Rio. He was just waiting for me to fuck up again.

"And how is this going to work exactly?" Dane demanded of Rio, as if I was invisible. *Sit there and shut up, Garrison. The grown-ups are talking.* "I assume you'll be rejoining Cage and the others at some point, and there's no way in Hell I'm letting you take Garrison with you."

"With respect," Rio answered, his tone turning frosty, "that's not your decision to make." He held up his hand, silencing Dane's protest before it could leave his lips. "Yes, I'm going back on tour, but I'm not taking Garrison. Not yet anyway. I hope he'll come out for the last couple of gigs in Canada, and then we'll fly home together. Until then, he'll be staying here."

Dane cast Riley a worried look. When Rio said 'here', Dane assumed he meant in London. The guy was torn between me and Riley again. Keep Riley happy and he faced losing me to suicide. Protect me, and he faced Riley calling it quits for good.

"I'll be staying *here*." I clarified to put him out of his misery. "At the cottage. All I'm asking for is a regular phone call and the occasional visit."

"So, you're not coming back to London?" Dane asked sourly. "You're just going to sit here, in Rio's house, getting drunk every minute of every day."

"It's Garrison's house," Rio said. "And there won't be any alcohol left on the premises when I leave."

"He'll go out and buy more, idiot." Dane paused. "Hold on, what do you mean, it's Garrison's house? Since when?"

"Since I gave it to him."

"Wow." Riley let out a low whistle. "We are so *not* in the same situation. I didn't get a house."

"You want a house? I'll buy you a house," Dane snapped, before turning back to Rio. "Look, I'm not happy about any of this. I know you're all loved up right now, but how long is it going to last? Until you cheat on him and shag one of your little groupies? Until Garrison goes on his next bender and tries to off himself again?"

"Hey, I'm sitting right here," I objected.

"Sorry. Garrison, but you know how I feel about this relationship. It's poisonous and it's not good for you. You need to come home, where I can take care of you."

"Yeah, because that's always worked out so well before." I took a deep breath and shook my head. It sounded like I was blaming Dane for all the times I'd cocked up or run away from him. "Dane, you're like a brother to me, and I love you, but you are not responsible for me. The drugs, the booze, fucking anything with a pulse, the suicide attempts... I did all those things. Not you. Most of the time, you weren't even there."

"Except for the one time I was," Dane blurted out. "And that one time is what led to everything else."

"What is he talking about?"

Rio tensed beside me, but I ignored him. I'd explain later, preferably when Dane wasn't around for him to kick off at. Right now, though, this was between me and Dane. And maybe a little bit Riley, who was staying schtum even though he was the one who wanted this conversation to happen.

"Dane, we did drugs together for two weeks. It's not your fault that you stopped, and I didn't. I have an addictive personality. Drugs, booze... it doesn't matter. I mean, I'm even addicted to Rio. You going to blame yourself for that too?"

"No, but... surely you can see how unhealthy that is for a relationship. Rio can't even make up his mind. He wants you. He doesn't want you. I can't keep up.""

"I'm a healthier choice than drugs or alcohol," Rio supplied dryly. "And, yes, it's taken me a long time to figure out what I want, but I know now. I want to be with Garrison. I'm good for him."

Dane snorted. "I think the bruises all over Garrison's body would say otherwise."

"Okay, that's enough. I happen to like my bruises. I *definitely* like him fucking my arse while he puts them there." this time, I was the one to raise a hand to cut off Dane's objection. "I'm sorry you disapprove, but my sex life is none of your business."

"I know, but..."

"Dane, you need to listen to him," Riley interrupted, laying a hand on Dane's arm. "He's trying to tell you something."

"Like what?" Dane

Grumbled, sulking now. For a man in his thirties, he could be childish at times. And for a supposedly smart man, he could act as dumb as fuck.

"Like you are not my keeper. You are not responsible for me, and you did not cause my multiple addictions. If you hadn't given me my first line of coke, somebody else would have. Only they wouldn't have had my back for so long after, and I want to thank you for being there for me." Dane looked a bit tearful, and I had to swallow the lump lodged in my throat before I could continue. It felt like we were breaking up. In a way, I guess we were, but it wasn't as if I never wanted to see him again. He was still my best friend and I needed him in my life, just maybe not on the overbearing level he was at now. "I know you don't understand the dynamic of our relationship, but Rio is good for me. I love him. And you love Riley, so it's time to concentrate on your own life and stop worrying about me. I'm Rio's problem now."

I snuck a quick glance at Rio, but he didn't seem bothered by my announcement. He watched Dane closely. Rio was probably angry to learn Dane had introduced me to drugs all those years ago, but he should also be grateful that Dane had stuck by me ever since. Unless there was more to it and, like Riley, he was jealous of mine and Dane's closeness. Maybe he couldn't wait to put distance between us.

"So, I'm supposed to just let you go?" Dane asked petulantly.

"Yes!" me, Rio and Riley all cried in unison.

To my relief, Dane's face creased into a smile. He'd never let me go entirely, but I didn't want him to. This was a new beginning for both of us, but it was also the end of an era. It didn't mean we had to cut out everything from our old lives, though.

"Fine, I'll back off, but that doesn't mean I won't be there if you need me." He stabbed a finger in Rio's direction. "And if you hurt him..."

"I won't," Rio promised.

"Give it a week or two and you won't even miss me," I teased. Although, he'd better miss me a bit or I was going to be deeply offended. "Spend more time with Riley. Buy him a house or something."

Riley blushed. "I really don't want you to buy me a house, Dane."

"Then write him a song," I said. "It worked for me."

Epilogue

I SAT at the end of the wooden jetty, the cool water washing over my bare feet. My guitar rested in my lap, and there was a notepad beside me, the pages rustling in the faint breeze.

Four months had passed since Rio signed his cottage over to me. I'd been sober, clean and clear headed the whole time. The songs I produced were finally worth more than the paper they were written on, and Dane was so keen to record them, he was talking about making back-to-back albums.

I missed Rio, but the depression I'd anticipated never materialised. He returned to America a couple of days after Dane and Riley's visit. We spoke daily on the phone or on Skype, once Riley gave me a crash course in how to use it. I wasn't so stupid as to indulge in cybersex, or whatever people called it, but I kept Rio's wank-bank topped up with steamy self-pleasure sessions for the spy camera in the bedroom.

So far, Rio had come home twice when Carnival had a break in their hectic schedule. We didn't spend *all* our time fucking each other's brains out, but it was a close-run thing.

In a few weeks' time, I would be flying out to join Rio for the last shows of the tour. I was nervous about seeing his bandmates again, although Rio assured me that they accepted I was going to be part of his life. Cage was cool with it and as he was Carnival's illustrious leader, the others were happy to follow his lead.

Mal was the exception, of course. Once Rio told Cage what Mal had done to me, and issued his ultimatum, Cage gave Mal his marching orders. They found an American bass player to finish the tour, so at least I wouldn't have to face Mal. If he was a nicer person, I might have felt sorry for him, but he wasn't so I didn't.

My phone rang, and I scooted back from the edge of the jetty before picking it up to answer. The last thing I wanted was to drop either my phone or the guitar into the water. This was probably the longest I'd ever held onto the same phone. Funny how sobriety made me less prone to losing stuff.

"Hey, I'm here. Don't hang up!" I practically yelled into the phone. "I was just…"

"Moving away from the water's edge," Rio said with a deep, throaty chuckle, "I knew that's where you'd be."

He worried at first, when he realised I spent most of my time sat at the end of the jetty. Eventually though, he accepted I had no intention of throwing myself into the river. It was simply my favourite place to be. Other than beneath Rio's naked body.

"Am I allowed to ask how your therapy session went?"

Rio always wanted to know. Sometimes I told him. Other times I didn't.

Doctor Hill was the best in his field, but our sessions could get pretty intense, and leave me feeling emotionally drained. I was lucky though, that he agreed to come to the cottage once every two weeks, instead of me having to make the trip to his London office. Finding out he brought his mistress with him, and they stayed in a hotel overnight before adding the cost to my bill, made it seem less of a charitable act, but I didn't care so long as he was helping me sort my head out.

"Today was good," I told Rio honestly. "He wants to work through some more shit before I join you. Says he can give me exercises to help me cope with being in a high-pressure social setting."

"Which is a good thing, right? I know Cage said he'd behave, but he's bound to be a dick at some point. He can't help himself."

"Yeah, but I'm sure I'll cope." Cage *was* a dick a lot of the time, but we'd been friends once and part of me hoped we would be again in the future. "Maybe we should hook him up with Doctor Hill. See if he can sort his life out before he turns forty."

"Never going to happen," Rio retorted. "Cage is a lost cause. Enough about him, though. You know what time it is?"

I smiled. Every phone call, every video chat, ended the same way – with me singing his song to him. Rio never seemed to tire of hearing it, even though mine wasn't the greatest voice in the world.

"Aren't you bored of it yet?"

"Nope, and I never will be."

I put the phone on speaker and carefully set it down on top of the notebook. Then I began to play.

"You say you can't be my happiness. You know that's not all that you are..."

"Garrison."

My fingers froze on the strings and my throat seized. He'd never stopped me before. Had I done something wrong?

"I want to be." His voice sounded far away and tinny over the phone.

Yet strangely close. Like there were two of him. Why could I hear two of him?

And why did one of them sound like he was standing right behind me?

I turned slowly.

Rio was at the end of the jetty, down on one knee with an open ring box in his hand. His beautiful blue eyes were uncertain, like he was questioning whether he was doing the right thing. Or maybe it was because he was afraid I would say no.

"Shouldn't you be in Seattle?"

"Yeah, Cage is spitting feathers. Darby is filling in for me for a couple of days. Thing is, I got this crazy idea in my head, and I didn't want to wait. I had this whole speech in my head and now I can't remember jackshit, so bear with me, okay." He sucked in a steadying breath. "I've loved you since the first moment I saw you. I think it was the same for you."

I nodded, unable to speak for the tightness in my chest. Fuck. I'd better not be having a heart attack. Not when I was seconds away from getting everything I wanted.

"Only for some messed up reason, neither of us could admit it, and all we did was hurt each other. I don't want to hurt you anymore, Garrison. I want to be your happiness. So... how about it? Want to get hitched?"

Choking out a 'yes', I threw myself into his arms. Rio onto me like there was no tomorrow. Which there had bloody better be now we were officially spending the rest of our lives together.

"Shit," Rio said, when we finally came up for air. "I hate books that end with the main characters getting married in the final chapter."

"That's okay. Our story isn't a book. It's a song."

"Yeah, sorry. I think you'll have to rewrite *Song for Rio*."

"I'll write you another song. I'll write you a million songs." I laughed, admiring the plain silver band he pushed onto my finger. "Because this isn't the final verse, Rio. Our song isn't finished. It's only just beginning."

The End

# Other Books by Kay Ellis

<u>Contemporary</u>

Young At Heart

Judge & Jury

Judge & Executioner

First Contact

Fantasize

Little Freak

Tribute

Samael

<u>The Macho Series</u>

Macho

Starstruck

Princess

Jelly Belly

<u>Fantasy</u>

Fireheart

Dreamweaver

The Last Firebreather

<u>Short Stories</u>

Archie's Diner

Little One

Secret Santa